It's Handy When People Don't Die

and other stories

JOHN McARDLE

poolbeg press

First published 1981 by
Poolbeg Press Ltd.,
Knocksedan House,
Swords, Co. Dublin, Ireland.

Acknowledgements are made to *The Irish Press 'New Irish Writing'*, *The Drumlin*, *Best Irish Short Stories 2* and *Tears of the Shamrock* where most of these stories first appeared.

The generous assistance of An Chomhairle Ealaíon (The Arts Council) in the publication of this book is gratefully acknowledged.

Cover illustration by Robert Ballagh
Designed by Steven Hope

Printed by Cahill Printers Ltd.,
East Wall Road, Dublin 3.

Contents

The Kinkisha

'Come on, you beggar's get, come on,' Margaret whispered to herself.

The robin tested his balance, see-sawing twice on his legs; he twisted his head and looked at the apparatus, took an indecisive hop towards it, stopped, speared his head upwards in fright. Margaret held her breath. The robin corkscrewed its head to look around, its black eyes swollen with anxiety. 'Christ, he must have smelled me,' Margaret thought. 'Jesus, Mary and sweet Saint Joseph make him see it.' The robin zig-zagged cautiously towards the bread, hopping to the bottom of a dockweed leaf, assessing the position, hopping to another. Soon he was in the same leaf-gap as the bread and Margaret checked the feel of the cord around her fingers and tightened her thumb against it. She waited: she'd give him one more hop. When he took it she gave him another and then her whole body shocked into the movement of her arm as she pulled the cord. The sand-riddle swallowed the grass beneath it, but, by that time, the robin was already stinging a patch of blue between an ash and a sycamore and heading for a freedom of white cloud on the horizon. Margaret said frig it anyway, lay back on the grass, hardly noticing the hard stone between her shoulder blades, and closed her eyes. She could hardly keep from crying with anger and she pressed her canines together to keep her nostrils from trembling while inwardly she cursed the robin, her husband and God.

'Oh, Jesus,' she said finally, 'what if I can't get one?'

She let the anger die and felt quietness draining into her ankles. She stretched up her hand and lifted the stone from between her shoulders and left it down gently on the grass beside her, rubbing her middle finger absently around a hollow in its surface, examining its crevices with her thumb. Then she joined her hands around it and allowed its moisture to soak into her warm palm. Lying like this she could feel the grass pushing through her shirt and she spelled the word June to see if there was an r in it — her grandmother always said not to lie on grass in a month with an r in it. She thought about the nights she lay under these trees with Gerry. On one of the nights, when it was all over and they were tired, Gerry found a burr sticking to his sleeve. 'I'll keep it to have,' he said, and put it in his pocket. A while after they were married she asked him about it. He said he didn't remember it but it must have come off a bush or something; he often noticed them on the calves, he said.

Margaret sat up.

The shirt was sticking to her back so she pulled it away with her fingers and looked out at the sand riddle; she had almost forgotten about it. As she went out to it she pulled the old stockings over her hand so that her smell wouldn't be left on the riddle. When she reached it she hunkered, lifted one end of the riddle up and balanced it finely on the end of the stick, moved the cord a little nearer the top of the stick and slid it through her hands as she moved away — that way it wouldn't get caught up in the weeds and make a noise when she pulled it. She edged back between two thorn bushes and round a briar-clump, holding the string clear of the grass all the time. When she reached the far side of the briars she selected a sturdy branch near the top and laid the cord across it, checked that she could see through the gap in the briars to the bread under the riddle and settled herself back against the mossy stones of the ditch. A curse of a job this waiting, but it had to be done.

She was getting hungry and a wind-pain was gathering in her stomach but she didn't want to leave. She sat a little sideways on the stone and pressed, but nothing came so she got no relief. If she was at home she could have taken Andrews or something like that but Gerry didn't like her taking medicine. She asked herself what *did* Gerry like her doing; everything she did was wrong. Not that she could blame him; she was at fault as much as him because you couldn't flout God and expect everything to turn out well.

From the length of the shadows she thought it must be about seven or eight — milking time. He was likely effing her from a height for not being back to give him a hand. She felt a chuckle rising in her throat at the thought but she stifled it in case the robins might hear her and then she looked through the gap at the bread in case a rat

7

or something might be at it. There was a shadow
cutting the sand-riddle in half and this worried
her because she knew it would get dark under
the shadows before anywhere else and it would
be hard to see a robin in the dark grass. She con-
soled herself that the sun was still warm and there
was a bit of the day left. She started to pray that
she would get one and not have to come back
again the following day and, as often happened
with her prayers, her mind wandered and she
remembered her grandmother beside her bed in
the nursing home: 'God love you, Margaret,
say your prayers for a Kinkisha is a terrible worry
to have on you.' She had her eyes turned upwards
piously and she was talking in the whining voice
that she used when she was saying her prayers
or talking to the priest, bouncing her handbag up
and down on her knees with her two hands and
holding her back stiff as she always did when
she was saying something she didn't want to say.

'There's something about being born at Whit,'
and she told about Michael Mulligan who was a
Kinkisha too and was got dead one night under
his overturned tractor on a flat road and about
other people born at Whit whom death had come
to in strange ways. 'I'm not trying to annoy you,
Margaret, but I want to make sure you make the
cure before he's two months; if I was you I'd
like to be sure.' And she left, saying she'd pray
about it.

Margaret stopped thinking because she thought
she heard the twittering of birds, but it was far
away and it didn't get louder.

She took the stockings off her hands and started
to rub the insides of her bare legs. She pulled a hair

or two off them with her nails and then rubbed the spots because they were sore and she kept on rubbing them until the darker patches under her outside skin dappled her legs. She lay back and felt the blood throbbing into the place she had rubbed and she closed her eye and trained the gunsights of her knees on the bait. The sun's rays livened a couple of hairs on the inside of her thigh. She blew them as she used to blow the dead seeds of dandelions and counted to eight as she blew: 'One o'clock, two o'clock, three o'clock.' When they didn't fall off at eight she laughed hoarsely to herself and re-focussed her eye on the bread. The hair on her legs was getting longer, she thought. Time was she'd have been worried about it. That was before they were married when other men in the dancehalls fancied her; men who could sing or dance or talk well; but Gerry was the one she wanted because she could never be sure that he was fond of her.

Two dragon-flies which had flown in from the river were mating in a patch of sun in the briar-leaves and she watched them, unblinking. Then she was shaking her thin clear wings still wet from the water of the river, and the he was making wilder flutterings on top of her. Together they floated into the air, twisting and humming, making music like in a dancehall. Were they sweating or was the she quivering from pleasure or struggling against some pain; or was she afraid of being crushed against the hard grass or stuck through by the thorn of a briar? They came out of a gap between two briar-leaves and prodded down into the grass a few feet away, still flutter- ing, still singing, moving from side to side. And

9

then they flew up again, their wings like rainbows when they hit patches of sun among the leaves.

Margaret took a stick and killed the two of them and immediately regretted moving at all because she saw, out of the corner of her eye, a bird flying away from the vicinity of the sand-riddle. But it came back in a minute — a robin — flying in narrowing circles over the bread. It came to the ground a few feet from the poised sand-riddle and Margaret waited till it was pecking at the bread before she pulled the string and jumped up, her face reddening with delight. She leaped over the briars, scraped between the bushes and scythed the nettles and dockweeds with her legs, her breasts jumping inside her shirt as if beating time to the strong thrust of her shoulders as she ran in a wild dash to make sure that she had caught it. It was there all right, whipping itself upwards towards the small squares of light above its head, jumping around inside and screaming wildly, battering its wings sideways against the rough wood, beating itself frantically against the wire mesh of the riddle.

She put in her hand and took it out. It was sweating and warm in her hand. Its head was bleeding where it had bashed against the wire and one of its eyes was filming over with a white scum. It was quiet now, pumping in and out against her hand. She pulled a handful of grass and cleaned her hand where the robin had spattered it in its fright. She pulled the front of her shirt out of her skirt and dabbed the edge of it against the blood on its head and tried to rub the scum from its eye. She must have hurt it because it strained against her fingers and clawed her hand with its feet. She looked at its neckless head shrivelled into its body in fear, its wings paralysed by the tightness of her hand around it; she felt a wild urge to let it go and to hell with her grandmother and Gerry and the child she hadn't asked for anyway, but she held on to the life in her hand because it was her own life she was holding on to and she knew that if she let go she would be throwing away the chance of escaping from the sand-riddle of imprisonment which God had thrown around her, baited all the time by Gerry's blaming eyes, the sorrowful, pitying face of her grandmother; and she heard the voice of the priest again, 'I wouldn't worry about it being born at Whit; *pisreogai*, Margaret, *pisreogai*. But God has a funny way of making people aware of their folly, Margaret,' and she looked all around at the darkening trees, thinking she heard vague rumbling of voices or a hoarse throaty laugh.

The robin jumped in her hand and frightened her so, compromising her impulse to give it freedom: she tightened the bottom of her shirt under the band of her skirt, undid a button of her skirt and pushed the robin in. It was soft and downy against her skin, its feathers tickling her navel. It moved hesitantly along the rim of her skirt-band, its wing-tip drumming against her stomach, feeling her, testing the touch of her skin. She drew in her stomach muscles and the bird sagged a little lower into the tucks of her shirt, its head tingling the skin around the hollow of her stomach, its vibrations tensing the muscles around her pelvis, electrifying them so that they twitched involuntarily. She held her breath for a minute and closed her eyes and when she started to breathe again her breathing was deeper and hollower, filling her lungs, pushing her breasts in and out, the hard fabric of her shirt like work-hardened fingers moving across them and she moved her head from side to side because there was a purring in it and, with her pelvis still thrust forward, she put back her hand against an uprooted tree-stump and eased herself down along it and ended lying on the grass with the bottom of her skirt around her waist, her head resting on a rusty root which bent and rose to the movements of her head. The bird started to move upwards across her solar plexus, fingering the bottom of her ribs, exploring the place where her ribs joined, moving the sweaty palm of its breast against the soft sides of her own, pressing them, clawing them with its nails, easing carefully up the hollow between them till it pushed its head between two buttons of her shirt into the darkening light of the wood.

She lifted her hand and pushed the head in again and moved her elbows upwards along her ribs so that she pushed her breasts together and she folded her arms across them feeling the robin sobbing in the flabby pouch she had thus made for it, her own breath catching in her throat because of some afflicted affection. She didn't notice the eerie listening of the hooded trees or the sound of a fox whining for a lost mate because she was listening to the sound of voices in her own head, somebody saying 'No' and another 'Why not?' and both saying it again and then the heavy breathing of two people growing stronger and louder, another heavier voice saying 'God will forgive you' and then the crying of a child, and she tightened her arms around her breast and matched the robin's sobbing with her own.

She got up quickly, bending her neck to wipe her wet cheeks on her shoulders and ran up the crooked path out of the hollow. The tears in her eyes made weird dancing shapes from the trees above her as she ran up the grass-slippery slope still cluthching the robin tightly to her. She got through a gap in the ditch and out of the wood and just missed hitting a drill-plough angled sideways on the head-rig of a weedy potato field. She thought she heard her own footsteps coming after her and hurried on, crying aloud although by now she didn't know why. She heaved across the stile at the end of the head-rig and headed for the light two fields away. She was out of breath when she reached the back of the house and she stopped and allowed the trembling in her legs to ease and the sweat on her body to soak into her clothes. Eventually she stopped crying and her breathing was getting easier so, laying her shoulder against the cold stone gable of an outhouse, she put her hand into her shirt and pulled out the robin.

It was damper than before but not as frightened and she cupped her hands around it and stroked its bloodied head with her chin. She looked towards the small twelve-paned window where the light shone through but she didn't want to go in for a minute. Her head on a flat pillow of limestone jutting out of the wall, she looked upwards at a half-formed foetus of cloud floating across the face of the moon and on the road a half-mile of rushes away she heard a drunk singing his way home. She heard the cats crying like banshees across the countryside and beside her she heard the low grunting of pigs.

Quietly she went into the yard, held the robin in one hand and with the other she turned on the lagged tap along the wall. She bent to allow the cold water to trickle into the hollows of her eyes so as to take away the redness from them before she went in. Gerry must have heard the water dripping on to the stones because he came to the door and opened it.

'Is that you?' he said, peering into the dark.

She pretended she was drinking from the tap and she wiped her face with her sleeve before she answered him.

'It's me all right,' — what answer did he expect.

'Any luck?"

'I got one,' she said as she went up the street towards the door.

'What did she say?' her grandmother's voice came from inside.

'She got one.'

'Praise be to God.'

Margaret came up to the door keeping her eyes on the robin in her hand so as not to have to look straight at Gerry.

'It hurt itself a little on the riddle,' she said.

'You got it anyway,' he said. "The sow had suckers when you were away; I'm just after pulling their teeth with the pliers so that they wouldn't tear the tits off her. Fourteen she had. That child cried all day.' He looked at the robin again. 'I see it shit on your hand; it must be afraid.'

She went into the low kitchen with the buff wainscotting and yellow wallpaper. Grannie was resting her feet on the black ledge of the range and she turned round when Margaret came in.

'You'd better do it now and be done with it,'

she said. 'I'll go with you and see that everything's done right.'

She took her stick from the back of the chair and lifted herself to her feet. There was a pot of bruised potatoes on the middle of the floor and, as she passed it, she stooped and lifted a handful out of it and threw it on the stone flags of the floor. The dog came from under the table and started to eat them.

The grandmother opened the door into the bedroom. 'Don't turn on the light or you'll only waken him,' she warned. The child was breathing the heavy air of sleep in the wicker basket on top of the bed.

'Lift it over here.'

Margaret pulled the basket with one hand, still holding the robin in the other.

'Put it into its hands now and do it.'

Margaret lifted the baby's hand, put the robin into it and wrapped her hands around it. In the moonlight which came through the cob-webbed window she could see the baby's eyes covered only by the light-blue almost transparent skin that makes a young baby's eyelids. She looked down at it in the moonlight; its nose was getting straighter and its chin was lengthening a little and the flaky look had gone from his skin. 'Come on,' her grand-mother was nudging her, 'come on now, Hail Mary . . .' She waited for Margaret to pick it up but when she didn't the old woman said 'Come on' again and with the robin and the child's hand held between her own trembling hands Margaret said three Hail Marys while her grandmother droned alongside her. When she reached the end of them she didn't wait for the grandmother to prompt her any further but, of her own accord, she started to squeeze her two hands tighter together. The robin pushed out the ribbed feathers of his wings against her hand and started to squirm more than before, but she steadily increased the pressure and a choking, rattling sound started inside its body, racking upwards through it as far as its mouth and it swallowed it back again so that the whole body shuddered and vibrated with it. Margaret looked coldly at the small bloodied head beating back and forth against her thumbs, twisting around, beak opening and closing, throat swallowing its own cry-song. 'Get a newspaper or something; it'll destroy the bedspread,' she said as she put her shoulders behind the effort she was making and the robin's wheedling grew weaker as if it were coming from the distance of the wood and she felt the crunch of bone on bone as its frame began to break and then a sudden spew of half-digested things burst upwards from its craw.

'I think it's dead,'' she whispered.

'Keep squeezing anyway; it's got to bleed,' said the old woman.

She felt the robin's body cave in under the pressure, heard a gurgling sound as the gizzard, the lights, the heart oozed like red paste through a gap in his wing-coverts and the blood swelled out along with them and trickled slowly down her hand towards the baby's hand which she still held loosely under the robin's body. She squeezed again to lend the blood speed and it trickled into the baby's hand, down along its arm and dropped noisily from its elbow onto the old newspaper which the grandmother had laid there. When the blood became thick and glutinous from pulped matter she stopped pressing and said the other three Hail Marys while the old woman got a bowl of water and a cloth and wiped the child's hands clean. The shape of Margaret's fingers were in the squashed mass of saturated feathers that was left in her hand. She lifted the bottom half of the window and threw it outside. The cat, always alert to possibilities, sprang to it, sniffed it and examined it but went back into the shed again and fell asleep.

Margaret and Gerry made love that night — the first since they were married. In the middle of it Margaret said: 'I saw two dragon-flies at this to-day in the wood,' but Gerry grunted, not wanting to be diverted. After it was over she said 'I think we'll be happier now.' She lay for a minute looking at the darkened ceiling boards; beside the bed the child was rustling the wicker basket where he lay. She turned, aligned her body with Gerry's, ran her fingers along the hair on his chest and whispered 'I killed the dragon-flies.' But Gerry was asleep; or if he was awake he didn't pretend he was.

Bonds

But tonight he was splay-footed on the chair against the fire-wall and he said: 'Sit down, missus. Tonight I'm . . . '

She paused, standing.

'Tonight I'm filled with . . . I'm all filled tonight.'

She didn't make a joke about that.

'It's annoying me,' he said.

'What?' She sat down, propping herself with the brush on the floor.

'I remember Parnell.'

'Do you? That must be a long time ago.'

'And what's annoying me is the woman.'

'Had Parnell a woman?'

'My own woman; that's what's annoying me — her and Jane; Parnell had two women. Give us another drink; I'll give you the price of it again.'

Once the others were gone he never asked for another drink so she poured him one, letting the froth build high so that she didn't have to fill it too full.

'And the girls,' he said when he had the glass in his hand. 'Them girls. Christ, them girls: one, two, three, four, five, six, seven. Christ, them girls.'

'Drink up. You should be going home.'

'Home?' he said, looking around as if expecting to see it. 'Yes, I suppose I should be — I should be — I should be going home.'

'My back's nearly broken and I have to open in the morning again.'

'Well then, I'll see you first thing in the morning.'

She got up to open the door but he stayed sitting near the fire. The night was on the window and the air of black frost blew in the open door. He didn't seem to notice that she had opened it.

'Martha, Mary, Millie — what age is Millie? Near fifty; near fifty is right, where does the time go to? Where does — Margaret, Madge and May. One after another, close the door, there's a draught.'

The widow closed it and stayed beside it. 'It's cold,' she said. 'There's a frost.'

'Frost is right. The sheep'll all be going down to the valleys. Every last one dropping down, one after another dropping down.' He raised his hand and his head and when he let them go limp they fell.

'Plop,' he said. 'All going down.'

He waited a while, almost snoring, and he said plop seven times and then he said: 'Do you see the stones in the old graveyard on top of the hill below? That's history there, you know; history.'

'There's people buried there,' she said.

'They're flagstones. There was lichen on them the last time I was down there. They're like old men's teeth,' he said. 'Old men's teeth. Not like mine because mine are good, but like the teeth of men that don't drink. I remember them short in the time of Parnell, the stones. I do, I . . .'

He put his head on his chest, looking towards the fire as if he saw something in it. The widow put out the middle light and the brown of the bar was dark in the light from the window.

'You'll be buried there yourself soon if you don't take care of yourself,' the widow said.

'You're a nice woman, missus, but I won't be buried there. I'll be buried with my own woman under the white stone with the gold on the top of it in the new graveyard. That's where —' He stopped and thought again.

'I have to get up early,' she said again.

'Then I'll see you first thing in the morning.'

This time she didn't move.

'You have all my money, missus,' he said.

'I haven't. It buried a whole family.'

'Wherever it's gone it didn't rear mine. All the time when them girls were young — Martha and Mary and Millie and Margaret — all them when they were young, and I hope I don't offend you, missus, but I hadn't the price of knickers for them, and when the wind was blowing or a frost like tonight —'

'They did grand.'

'Grand.'

'Yes indeed.'

'Yes.'

She sighed, sagging, and yawned. 'Indeed they did.'

'Well I reared them right. Upstanding lassies.'

She went to the window. The lights had gone out in bedrooms all over the mountain and there was only the hulking shape of the peak against the sky and the single light in Tom's house.

'They'll be waiting for you,' she said. 'They're

still up.'

'They always are,' he said. 'They can't go to bed because if they did I'd waken them to say goodnight. Every last one of them, one after another — plop, plop, plop — one after another; that's the way they dropped from the woman's inside — one after another — plop. Jaysus, missus, she was a great woman; a big woman; a big strong woman that you'd take a lease on her life. Plop.'

'Drink up.'

Before he started to raise the glass he put back his head and opened his mouth. He emptied it into his mouth, gave a few gurgles and, when he was leaving it down, something between a breath and a cough. The frost was a bitch, he said, and the snow. He remembered the rocks when there was only a little bit of them over the ground but two thaws came after two big snows and the ground slipped away from the bottom of the stones. The year of the first thaw the girls left him. 'It was the snow; and the wind blowing the frost into holes. When I think of all them holes and not a stitch on them' — that's why they said they were leaving; Martha divided their mother's clothes among them; too big for the wee ones, too small for — 'Some of them loose in them and some of them tight in them. But they took after their mother; they had looks.'

The first of them came back in a piddly. The sobs racked up his throat. 'The first bloody one I had to christen on my own and I made a balls of it.'

He cried for a long time then and a hand moved unknown to him and swept the glass from the table. The widow wiped up the floor and picked up the pieces of glass and she allowed the froth to settle on the next one so that she could fill it to the brim.

'You'll be all right,' she said. 'Women, once they're dead, don't mind what their children are called.'

It was a long time before he was able to stand and his trousers were twisted when he got up. She helped him to straighten them and she helped him to the door. When he was sitting on the step she closed the door and hurried to her bed.

Although it was cold he sat there most of the night, unable to move. He could see the light in his brown house on the other side of the valley but he couldn't make himself move towards it. He said goodnight to himself a few times and tried to sleep. The frost gathered on the pub windows and the tail of his coat stuck to the door. When he finally moved with the dawn he went only to where a rocky corner cut the pub from his sight. He sat in the middle of the road, afraid of falling down some of the steep banks on its side and, sitting there, he noticed cold foxes tricking about in the heather. The grey houses were blue in the valley and the chiselled stones were sloped.

He took courage and moved when the sun began to come up, himself and the sun holding to the high rocks along the road so as not to have to fall into the valley. Crossing the bridge before starting to climb again he stopped to open his mouth to the mist of the river's spume. The sun was at his house long before him.

Still Martha had a candle in her hand when she came to the door.

'Where were you?'

'Ssshhhh.'

'We're up all night.'

'Then it's bedtime. Where's Jane?'

He searched for her among the seven faces inside.

'Jane,' he said. 'Kneel at my feet.'

He sat on a stool and she came and knelt with her hands on his knees. The others gathered around, sitting on the floor beside them. He took off his wattled overcoat and rolled it up before he spoke.

'Jane,' he said. 'You can hang up my coat tonight.'

He held it to her with both hands and she smiled at him and took it. As she got up she hugged it to her breast. She stood looking down at him and he raised his head and he looked at her face for the first time.

'You have looks,' he said.

She turned away and the others moved to make a path to the nail. When she had it hung up she didn't turn around again but stood with her back to them, stroking it.

'I'm taking my supper in bed tonight,' he said, to break the stillness.

The sticks on the fire were bright and the porridge was hot. It was Margaret's turn to hand it to him and they followed her into the bedroom to say goodnight. His was the highest of the eight beds and he was sitting propped by the grey pillow. Before he took the tray he said: 'Whenever I go back to your mother I'll be able to tell her how well we all got on.'

They sat, each on her own bed, and when he had

finished the porridge they gathered around him.

'I'll see you all some time,' he said before he closed his eyes and fell asleep.

In a while he snored and talked a little. Puzzled and afraid, the girls made work for themselves around the bed, tightening loose tassels on the quilt or smoothing ruffles near his feet, trying to hide from each other the blot which each felt was on the happiness of the forgiveness. He was serene and in a deep sleep and the wood-shadow of the morning on the window was moving towards the edge of the pillow. If they had to talk they talked in whispers because they knew that, even if he lasted the day, he couldn't have many years to live.

With the lowering of the sun's cross on the bed they decided not to sleep but to wait again for the night. While he slept they moved in and out to the porridge-pot, dallying over it with light talk. Towards noon they began to talk in whispers about their husbands and children in Birmingham and Coventry and by the time the sun crossed the bottom of the bed to die on the wall by the door, Margaret, Mary, Millie, Martha, Madge, May and Jane admitted to themselves and to each other that some day not far away they would each have to go back again to living with an ordinary man.

The Light's Edge

Jem gathered a wet thread from his overcoat sleeve around his hand and cut it with his teeth. Better be rid of that. The sleeve was well-ravelled, threads going every way and him breaking off a bit every couple of days. He'd have to get someone to sew it — some neighbour woman. Three years only he had this coat and it starting to wear already. Long ago a coat used to last him and last him for years and when it was finished it lasted him for a few more years for frosty mornings outside. Bad stuff in coats nowadays.

He reached through its torn pockets, loosened his belt one notch, and back-handed, pushed his shirt down over a cold spot, gave it a rub of his hand to warm it and tightened his belt again. He stood, maybe to rest himself, maybe to look around at the cold hills turning khaki with the withering grass and ripened potato stalks. 'Thirty days have September, April, June and November,' twenty-nine days to Christmas — no wonder the grass was beginning to wither — ripening and withering, 'much the same, aren't they.' He turned his back to the icy wind to look back at his own brown hill with six pits of potatoes — two straight rows of three. They looked longer in the thin light — six big pits ten foot long every one of them, except the wee one, and it took him only a week to dig them. 'Begod they'll be starting to grow again before Pete gets finished,' he laughed to himself as he turned into the wind and faced Pete's hill. Look at the way he dug them — a wee patch here and another there as if he thought he was getting on better that way, and he took a cup of tay between every few stalks to give himself an excuse for a rest — a bit lazy, Pete was, maybe. But all right. Pete was all right. All the same he should fix that footstick and put a railing along it to catch on to — and he should have taken in that spade and not leave it out all night. 'Them's the spuds that'll take a long time to dig. In the end he'll wind up giving good money to Deery or some big farmer with a digger and two big horses.'

He rubbed something clammy from his moustache and followed the winding path between the white-topped rushes. The path was well worn with him going over to Pete and Pete coming over to him and it was already getting hard with the night's frost. Jem put his hand round to his back and rubbed a painful spot. His legs were getting sore too, now that he was getting cold. It was hard work digging and gathering. Some men had women to gather and it left it easier. When he was young and strong he'd have dug that field in three days and danced on the third night. No pains then. Not much sense either. But you didn't need sense if you were a wild devil because if you were a wild devil people took you like that and made allowances. That was when he was young. Young and

26

wiry. In the middle of his young strong days.

The accordion-player struck up a creaking waltz.
Jem kicked a loose stick into the bonfire, cheered,
and swaggered over to Mary McCabe. Pete just
got there as he reached her so he cheered again,
hit him a shoulder and landed him among the shawl-
ed women leaning against the earthen ditch.
Pete picked himself up, lifted his cap from Mrs.
McBennett's lap and with three sharp strides
vaulted through the flames into the bunch of
lassies on the other side. He picked one out and
whisked her to the centre of the crossroads where
he bumped into Jem again.

'Did I see you somewhere before?'

'Get outa my road.'

'Here, Pete, surely you can squeeze her tighter
than that,' and he pushed them closer together.

'Were you not listening to Father O'Kelly on
Sunday, were you not, you heathen you? I always
say there's one thing about Father O'Kelly, you
can't play poker on the chapel steps and listen
to him at the same time.'

'Put in your shirt-tail.'

'And give me back that shirt tomorrow morning.
I don't mind lending them but I like to get them
back. And mind that woman for me. I'll want
her back too when you're finished with her.
Yahoooo,' and he buck-leaped into the middle
of a bunch of girls.

Jem watched him over Mary's shoulder. Pete
turned round, now surrounded by girls as he liked
to be and shouted something which Jem couldn't
catch in the swaying rhythmic kicking of pebbles
and chattering voices rising above the creaky notes

of the huddled musician. Jem laid his elbow on Mary's shoulder to loosen the second button of his shirt, and he felt how soft her shoulder was and how three strands of auburn hair tickled his forearm.

'Hello,' he said as if he hadn't noticed her before.

'Hello. You're back?'

'Back.'

'Maybe it's soon be over.'

'Hope so.'

'Where next?'

'I'm not supposed to tell.'

'Do you not be afraid?'

'Wicked sometimes, when you're waiting for them to come along. Too much time to think.'

'It might be soon over.'

'It might.'

He eased her into the shadow where the flickering fire lit her face with a red orange glow. 'It might. I hope it does.' He looked back through the dancing haze between the flames where he could see Pete lift two girls by the waist. Jem kissed her. She didn't say anything but looked at him. What odds if she was Pete's girl; she'd never marry him anyway; women liked solid farmers with fifty acres or a braggart like himself who lived nearer the edge of danger.

'We'll sit down, I think,' he said.

She sat on the dusty grass at the road's edge and laid her back against his shoulder for support. He looked at her white neck. She was there for the taking, he thought, and he wondered if he should.

'Hi, Pete,' he shouted, but Pete didn't hear him. 'Pete,' louder, and the noise faded in expectation.

28

'Give us a sword-dance.'
'No sword.'
'Use a stick.'
'No stick.'

Jem pulled one from the bushes and flung it to him.

'Right, me flower. Pat, wind her up,' and he whipped off his cap and whisked it through the flames and Jem caught it with his outstretched left hand. Mary was tapping her feet like the rest, tapping her feet and clapping her hands as Pete swayed and jumped around the stick, moving with imperfect rhythm to imperfect music. Clapping, tapping, cheering, lilting, dancing, and the armpits of Pete's faded blue shirt were turning green. It was under his armpits that Jem noticed the jiggering light on top of the brae. Everybody else had seen it too because the clapping stopped, the music faded, young men froze where they were and old women gathered their shawls around their breasts as if hiding infants. Over the crackling noise of the fire he heard the lorry.

'Tans,' someone whispered.

'For Jesus' sake, play on,' Jem shouted the whisper as he reached into the roots of the bushes for his gun, pulled it out and vaulted the ditch with one movement, and ran in wild panic through knee-deep dewy hay. He tripped on a stone and got up again. The music and dancing started again as he reached the river. He jumped it and landed in the soft ground on the other side. He felt a twitch in his ankle as he hit a stone under the muddy surface but he pulled his feet clear from the clinging earth and hurried through the rushes towards where a bushy ditch divided two hills black with whins. He jumped the ditch and almost collapsed as a sharp pain knifed his ankle. He limped on, dragging his right foot up the hill, till at the top he sank into a hollow in the earth, rolled over and landed on his back in damp grass. Lying on his back with his gun between his legs, its barrel facing towards his head, he tried to mute the sound of his heavy breathing. He sat up with his head between his knees and the gun over his shoulder. He lifted his head and looked through the bushes. The music had stopped again and shadowy forms moved between him and the firelight. After a while he heard the faint purr of the engine, saw the lights illuminate small bent figures heading homewards. The lorry moved off and he lay under a starry sky till the dew soaked through his shirt. He sat up to feel his already-swollen ankle. What was this, Pete's cap still clutched tightly in his fist. Pete was probably seeing her home now. Lucky for Pete. Buck him, he had nothing to fear from the Tans. 'He'll enjoy his freedom like the rest of us all the same.'

'Pete.'
    'Hello, Jem.'
    'Cool.'
    'Aye, cool is right.'
    'I wish it was your turn tonight but sure you came to me last night.'
    Pete was hanging the kettle on the crook and didn't answer.
    'I saw a rat eating haws off a bush today. Looks like a bad winter. That's always a sure sign of a bad winter.'
    He edged between a barrel of wet meal and a

table covered with pieces of bread, tin dishes and brown delph, and threw the cat from the top of the settle-bed to make room for himself.

'You got finished the digging I see.'

'Aye, just got it finished there before dark. Ah now, it's tough work digging. It's the stooping that gets you. In the back you know. I see you have rats.'

'They come in for the winter. The cat's clean useless — got a sort of used to them.'

'You should get Dak.'

'I got some one time and the cat got caught in it. I got her the next morning and freed her but she only lived a few days — strained herself or something.'

There was silence for a few minutes. It went on too long so Pete said 'Aye. I'd say she strained herself,' to fill the gap.

After another silence 'That kettle's not boiling. Give the bellows a blast and I'll make the tea.'

Jem moved into the corner at the end of the settle to turn the wheel.

'You should do something with them bellows. They're loose in the ground.'

'I was looking for blue clay at the edge of the bog there this evening. There was a great seam of blue clay there but I must have used it all.'

'It's bad for the bellows jigging about like that. It loosens all the screws in them and the next thing you'll find they won't blow at all.'

'I might buy cement the next day I'm in town.'

'Aye, mix it with a bit of sand and lime and it should do your job.'

Pete shook tea from the bag into the kettle and Jem blew the bellows again. Pete buttered

31

the bread, sugared the cups, poured the tea and handed the cup to Jem with two thick slices of bread on top. Jem hated that. The steam from the tea always wet the bread and he couldn't stand wet bread. There were brown streamers down the side of the mug so he rubbed them with his sleeve till they became a bigger patch of lighter brown, and started to drink.

'Great strong tay, Pete.'

'Nothing like it. Good tay and a good fire is all a man wants.'

'Begod that's a powerful fire all right. You'd make a great divil, Pete.'

'Aye, or a purgatory.'

They smiled and went solemn again.

'Purgatory wouldn't be too bad, Pete.'

'I suppose not.'

'But I wouldn't like Hell. Purgatory would only last for a wee while.'

'A man told me once that you might have to spend a brave while in it.'

'I don't know. I suppose so. You heard Mary Deery died today.'

'God be good to her.'

'Died about twelve, I think. It was the creamery man that was telling me.'

'She was failed this last few years.'

'Got very grey and pale.'

'Shockin' grey. She used to have lovely auburn hair.'

'A brave woman.'

'Ah God, aye. A lovely woman. She shoulda never married Deery.'

'Not at all.'

'God be good to her.'

It ended at that. For a moment they were left alone with their thoughts. Separate. Pete coughed and said 'I see you got finished the digging.'

'Aye, just got it finished before nightfall. It's hard work digging — on the back, you know — with the stooping.'

'A good crop you had.'

'Six big pits. That's a great field, Pete. I mind selling seven tons off that field one time. Seven tons of Aran Banners that'd melt in your mouth.'

'I'd rather Kerr's Pinks myself. They're a better yielding spud.'

'Ach, they're a weak sort of spud. Not much body to them. Them Aran Banners had a flouriness. Boil them and you had half an inch of flour before you came to the heart.'

'But they're a rough spud. A rough skin on them. A Kerr's Pink — did you ever see the way you could peel a Kerr's Pink with your nail or even a rub of your thumb and you had the skin off it.'

'They're a bad spud, Pete.'

'No, now Jem, there's nothing like them.'

'A bad spud.'

'No.'

'Aran Banners from the Aran Islands. Give me them any time.'

'But they're a rough spud.'

'Give me Aran Banners from the Aran Islands. Them other ones is a British spud and you'd know it.'

'They're a good fine spud.'

'They're watery.'

'They're not watery.'

'They're watery — like the British.'

'I wasn't trying to start politics.'

33

'Doesn't matter. They're a watery spud. Dead watery.'

'I wasn't . . .'

'Doesn't matter.' And Pete didn't answer.

Jem knew he shouldn't have bothered. Pete was all right. He shouldn't have argued with him. Dammit all there wasn't much use in fighting at this stage of their lives because Pete wasn't a bad fellow. He got on your nerves betimes, but you'd be lonesome without him. Like in the snow when he couldn't cross the footstick for fear of slipping and you had to spend the long dark night on your own. No, begod, fair play to him. Pete was all right. A bit thick, but all right. He'd say he was sorry. He'd swallow his pride and say he was sorry. He stretched out his legs and drew in a big breath to prepare himself, and said 'That's a powerful fire,' but Pete didn't answer.

Pete didn't answer. No use saying any more. But he should have answered. If you said something to somebody they should answer. No use talking if they didn't answer. But he'd sit it out because if he left now Pete mightn't come over the next night and then next night he wouldn't go to Pete and it could go on like that into the long winter — winter nights with a candle and a cat, one after another till spring — if you ever saw spring. You could go to McCabe's or Lennon's but you didn't know whether they wanted you or not, they'd maybe turn the wireless on and you were afraid to talk. No. Pete'd come round in a wee while.

A clock hurried across the floor. Jem hit it with his stick and smashed it and threw it into the fire. It disappeared in the flames. A clock. There was an English fella one time home in Lennon's that used to call them cockroaches. A tweedy wee fella with riding breeches and a moustache. A bit of a cockroach himself. No sign of it now. No sign of the clock. Gone into the flames, the leaping flames climbing up the black bricks to escape the white heat in the heart of the fire, jumping up to catch the crooks. A lovely white heart, a wee world in an empty space with the sun shining. Shining bright and warm, taking away the pains from his legs and shoulders — digging without effort, no pain from digging — bend down, give the spade a twist, shake them away from the stalks, lift them into the bucket. No trouble. Ten drills dug already but you'd have to watch the spuds so they'd stay in the pit. That little beggar was escaping, get back, batter it back, back, back, there now you little brat. A Kerr's Pink — you'd know it, you wee watery brat. Back to the digging and stay there you, stay there. Damn your soul you wee watery brat with your moustache and riding breeches — 'Ha, Pete, he used to call them cockroaches.' Pete didn't answer. He looked over at him but he was sitting there with his eyes closed looking into the fire. He couldn't leave now. He'd have to sit it out. Sit it out on this cold hill with the rain beating down on him soaking his uniform. Where the hell did the other lads go to? He was afraid himself but he wouldn't leave one man to fight them on his own. God knows who it was waiting for him — maybe his own trying to surround him, closing in on him. There he was. That one coming through the whins. Come on. Come on. Come on me boy and you'll get what you're looking for. Come on. He felt someone else behind him and he turned with his gun ready but the man took off his cap and floated it through the haze over the fire. he might be an enemy or he might be a friend. Jem caught the cap with his left hand and the force of catching it knocked him down into the furze between the apple-trees. It could be a friend. There was sound around; the sound of the wind. But not here. Not here in the hole where Aran Banners from the Aran Islands fell from the furze onto the ground. It was safe here from the sound of guns. And warm because the sound of the wind went over your head. Something scurried across his foot and he sat up in the chair.

He was cold. He shivered and drew the coat across his chest and tightened the cord round the middle. He poked the ashes with his stick and one spark rose and died. The lamp was gone out — a good job because it saved oil — but the chimney corner was beginning to brighten. The clock in the window said a quarter to six and behind it the sky was brightening. Another cold day. He knew from the breeze that came under the door and the white frost on the small window-panes. A rat was scratching in the low corner — rats used a slower, heavier stroke than mice. He rubbed his legs to get a bit of heat into them. Very quiet it was at this time of the morning — nothing only a rat scratching and Pete's heavy breathing. Pete'd have a sore neck when he wakened, the way he was sleeping with his head back and sideways on his shoulder. He made to move him but stopped. He'd only waken and it wouldn't be fair — he'd only be mad with him again. He turned as quietly as he could, took two turf from beside the fire, put them on the ashes and poked the ashes with his stick. He went over and lifted the top of the settle-bed, shoved in his arm and pulled out the first thing he met — a grey army coat — and laid it on Pete's chest and let it fall down over his knees. He got a queer feeling that Pete was looking at him because Pete always slept with one eye open — some disease he had when he was a gasun Pete always said. At the end of the jamb he stopped to look back. Pete was snoring now and beside him a small flame was feeling the bottom of one of the turf. It'd be a good fire when Pete'd waken.

He gathered his coat collar round his neck and up to his chin, lifted the latch and went into the dirty street with dirty white-washed outhouses and a lone bush growing in the middle of it. A cool morning with hens beginning to cluck on the roost. A frosty morning. Pete'd be warm enough in a wee while when the fire got lit up. It'd likely light up nice and red. Pete'd be all right — nice and warm. A funny man, Pete. Terrible thick. But all right.

It's Handy When People Don't Die

One evening in the summer Art saw her with the Cobbler That Had Time To Talk. Her skirt was white and she was brown with the sun. In the middle of a patch of grass on the side of the mountain he put his hand on her stomach and the two of them lay looking at the sky. The autumn came after the summer and then the leaves left the whins, so Art had a long time to think of that day. Sometimes, thinking about it, he was so happy at her getting a good man that he cried. One day The Cobbler saw him crying and he told Art he'd give him a horse some time instead of her.

The Cobbler That Had Time To Talk died when snow was on the mountain. Even for the time of year it was cold in the hard east wind and bad weather to get killed in. The crowd was round the house; men inside the burned-out walls gathering bits of the Cobbler into the coffin. The wind was sticking people's clothes to their legs. It was the same with The Brown Girl: the shape of her in her skirt where the wind pushed against her clothes.

'Bad weather's right,' Art said to himself, sheltering in the crowd. 'Maybe it's no time to be looking at the wind.'

The horse was shivering in front of the slipe, waiting for The Cobbler to be loaded. Art went round all the people, stooping down where they stopped the wind, and he said hello to them. Because The Cobbler talked to Art, people cried when they saw him at the funeral and one man said 'You lost an ould friend' to him. He noticed that where The Brown Girl stood the horse blocked the worst of the wind and he pushed through the crowd and stood beside her, looking at her crying.

'Hello,' he said. 'It's a pity about The Cobbler.'

Her face tightened, but she said nothing.

'Because he'll never marry you now,' he said.

She started to cry worse and bent her head and rested on her father. The father said with his moustache 'He was the same age as you, Art.'

Everybody was nice to Art that day. Rain came when the men carried the coffin out from the black walls and Art stood in the middle of the path the people left between the coffin and the slipe. He said 'Right a bit, left a bit, whoa, stand back there,' and walked backways in front of the coffin. When it was left on the slipe he heard somebody saying that The Cobbler was forty.

'Too bad about the Cobbler. Me and him's the one age,' he said to the slipe-driver. The slipe-driver looked at the coffin and tipped the horse with the tether. It moved off over the mountain pass, stretching with the weight of the hill, and Art walked in the shelter of the people through the next valley with a lake in it and through two more valleys to where a grave was opened beside a chapel

39

in a hollow. The Brown Girl fainted at the grave and was carried back in the slipe. Art saw the end of The Cobbler That Had Time To Talk through the shovels of clay, and he went home to hang forty sticks from the thatch of his house and another one that he put a notch in. Every day after that he put a notch in the stick that told him his age to the day.

That day was the dead of winter and the weather improved from there. There was talk about a rising and fighting. Men sat on stones. 'Father Murphy says not yet, but he thinks we should fight all right.'

'When The Cobbler was killed was the time.'

Art sat and listened to them without them noticing him and, from the valley where people were, he watched his lambs growing on the mountain.

'Who got The Cobbler's land?'

Four of the neighbours was all it was divided among and some people that didn't get any thought that they should have. The Brown Girl stayed inside until after Easter and one day she came out to work the bit of The Cobbler's land that her father got. Crops started to grow in The Cobbler's land and, by the time the summer came again, rain had washed his walls white. The Brown Girl didn't talk much to the men that talked about The Rising.

'I don't know what they're fighting for,' a cripple said as he was wheeled along the slipe-track in a wheelbarrow. 'There was never a Rising won before and look what The Yoemen did to The Cobbler.' Art heard all the talk sitting between potato ridges and he heard them talking more about The Cobbler.

'He was still alive when they burned the house. People heard him roaring but were afraid to go out.'

Men That Were Told That told men that he ran after them on one leg and they threw him back into the fire. Men put bits to it till Art couldn't remember how it was told in the beginning.

'Bad boys them Yoemen,' he said, one day, to men that were talking.

'If they get you, Art, they'll eat you alive,' and they laughed.

'Christ, bad boys, I'm telling you. If they get yous either yous won't be laughing.'

But that was one of the few times he talked; the men made more sense when they were talking to themselves and he was listening. Sometimes the Brown Girl passed, maybe with a bucket or a hoe, and if the men were laughing they put down their heads and stopped; and Art, doing the same, learned to look at her under his eye.

No matter what The Cripple said, Father Murphy came for the men. One time when they were sitting on stones, talking about crops, word came for them to get ready and they gathered around the rock in the middle of the valley that Art called the belly-button. They had their bags of belongings at their feet; their pikes in the air like corn. 'Hail Mary full of grace,' and all that from the women. Art sat between two rocks at his house, his pike in his hand and his oatcake crumbling against his chest, not feeling like going down to listen to what they were saying. 'They'd pick outa me about what the Yoemen would do.' Father Murphy came over the far side of the mountain. When he came to the ridge before the last slope Art put the shaft of the pike in his armpit, held the oatcake with both hands and, racing Father Murphy to the belly-button, tumbled down the mountain to the valley. 'I'm a terrible fella, leaving the sheep,' he said. The blade of the pike trailed the rocks and made like horse's dust along the slipe-track and, by the time he reached the men, it was cabbered like a set of teeth and the point lay sideways like a dead man's head. He stood it up on the heel of its shaft like the rest of the men. It was as long as any of theirs.

Father Murphy's horse was a ringle-eyed bay with a star on its forehead and white spots on its belly and its mane hanging halfway down its neck. His chest bulged and he rippled it to chase away the flies. He was strong enough to carry two men as big as Father Murphy, big and black on top of him, up as high as the top of the pikes and his hair flying out from the wind of riding.

'They burned the chapel.' he said, almost whispering. 'Now's the time to fight.'

He stopped, looking round the men, as if looking for their faces to answer him.

'Righto then, off we go,' Art said.

None of them moved. The priest put his elbows on the horse's neck and lay closer to the men.

'There's no more to be said. May God give strength to your arms and keep you safe.'

He lifted his hand and the men knelt down. He blessed them and turned his hand and they stood up. A pull of the reins and a tip of his heels and the horse galloped away from them. They followed it with The Brown Girl's father in front, marching like a Yoeman. The women kneeling along the slipe-track got up to hug them and cry for them, but they were all so busy crying for their own that none of them noticed that Art was going. He ran to the front of the men and shouted 'A bit to the right, a bit to the left, whoa, stand back there,' and he saw The Brown Girl and the other women looking at him. The Brown Girl's father came up to him and put his hand on his back.

'You'd better go back to the back, Art, in case we're attacked from behind,' he said.

'Righto so.'

He walked backways after the men going up the slope and, as they went over the top of the mountain, the women started to move back to the houses. He stopped to watch them moving out like a star, heads bent down with loneliness. They moved out, not talking to each other, gathering children around their legs like chickens; the Brown Girl on her own with her fat mother. By the time she went into the house the men were past the lake in the next valley. He gathered his oatcake against his chest and ran after them.

At the lake he got tired and stopped to rest. Rocks grew out of the lake beside bushes and he sat on one of them dangling his feet in the water. There were fish in it; no hurry on them. He studied them moving around green things at the bottom of the lake. And then he died.

He was at the back of a rock when his head went sideways on to his shoulder, his eyes closed and he fell with his stomach on the rock. His head fell upside-down over the water lapping there. He grunted and moaned. Dribbles from his mouth ran over his eyes and down into his hair. Breath came tired and hard. He said an Act of Contrition to himself, trying to mean every word of it, trying to imagine God waiting for him above, looking forward to seeing him. 'Oh God I am heartily sorry . . .' The Brown Girl's face came in front of his closed eyes. '. . . for all my sins because they offend you.' The wind was inside the rock that his ear was against and there was a half-notion of water inside it. He gave a little cough and went still.

Lying upside-down he said 'It's not that bad. If I had to die again I wouldn't mind it.'

Not but it seemed to annoy the women of the valley and make them cry.

He sat up and put his feet in the water again. The sun moved the shadow of the mountain onto him and the bright bellies of the fish got clearer. He ate the oatcake and thought about the men and how hard it would be to catch them now.

'I'd have to run too hard. It's coming to dark and I'd never find them.'

He decided not to bother. He followed a hooting owl home to his own dark and quiet valley with no lights in the houses and he climbed the whins and rocks to his house. Lying in the straw of his bed with the gashed blade of the pike at his head he heard the sticks rattling in the breeze that came under the door. He cut a deeper notch in the last one to show the day he went to be a soldier.

In the next days he could see his lambs growing bigger, getting themselves ready to be killed. Fine lambs. From the mountain hollow behind his house where he ate cuckoo sorrell he could see them hanging on the rocks. Lying there one day, a frog jumped across him and he caught it before it hit the ground. He blew it up with a straw and, when it burst, it reminded him of The Cobbler and he thought of how mad the women would be when the corpses all came back and he wasn't among them. 'I'd better hide from them,' he said. There was no telling what they'd do with him if they saw him, so for days he walked around the house on his hands and knees and watched the women from between the two rocks in front of the door. One evening prayers came up from the valley and he hurried to the rocks waiting for a corpse. There was none. The women were kneeling round the belly-button praying at candles they'd lit on it and when they went into the houses for the night they left them blazing there. The Brown Girl was the last to leave them, praying longer than the others. She walked across the valley in her white dress when the chilliness of the night was coming on.

In the middle of the night he visited the candles and named them after men from the valley — one for every man that left and one for himself — fat ones with dripping tallow for fat men and thin ones for thin men. His own was ordinary, on a nice stand. If he waved his hand they flickered and if one went out he lit it again. Going home, a butter-fly passed him. He lost it in a yellow whin where, sitting, he thought it was safer for a butterfly to be out in the dark when it couldn't be seen. 'I'll sleep in the day and walk the mountains at night,' he said, and he shuttered his windows and lit a fire to roast potatoes when the smoke couldn't be seen in the night. At the end of some nights and days he saw a darker one with thicker mist and, when he was going down to annoy the candles, he took a tub with him. There was a goat tethered to a post at the top of a hollow near the belly-button. He waited in the hollow till she grazed round the end of the rope and, holding her by the horns, he milked her with one hand. A corpse came into the valley before it was right bright and he thought it would be too risky to milk the goat again.

The corpse belonged to The Brown Girl's father. He came back into the valley with his hat a little sideways on his head, swaying on the horse as if he was drunk, but a proud man trying not to fall. He came slowly down the mountain pass, the horse careful not to fall on the twirly stones. His coat swung in the warm wind. Whoever killed him knocked the pipe from his mouth because no puffs of smoke followed the horse that he rode.

'Christ,' Art said when he saw that.

Women and children came out of the houses to look at him. He lay back, not smoking, straight and looking alive. At the level ground at the bottom of the mountain the horse lifted his head and went loose, nodding on towards the belly-button. But, instead of going there, the corpse pulled the horse in at his own front door and the big man riding behind him got off. The corpse fell down on the horse's mane as if he was crying. The Brown Girl came out screaming and her mother waved her arms. The big man lifted the Brown Girl in his arms and carried her inside and, after a while inside, the mother came out again and stood under the horse's head. Maybe she was crying, because she and the corpse were noted for getting on well together, but Art was too far away to see.

The women from the houses moved closer into a ring as the rider humped the corpse on his shoulder and carried him into the house. The ring tightened to the door and the women bent down to listen but they seemed afraid to go too near. The big man came out, looking back into the house. No Brown Girl yet. Not even the mother came out as the horse wagged its tail over the mountain to the next valley and when it was gone Art could see it no more. Now there was nothing to look between the rocks at except the women kneeling round the door; likely saying Our Fathers and Hail Marys and Glory Be To The Fathers. 'How's she taking it?' he said to himself. 'Through time she'll be lonely, I'd say.' But not yet because now she had plenty of company. It was the days when all the men were gone and the talk of the dying was over that he was afraid of.

For now all the stir was still on. The women were running around carrying basins and kettles of water that he hoped wouldn't scald The Brown Girl's father. The bed for the dead that the valley owned was taken to the house, white clothes were taken between the houses to make him look well when the people came in to watch him dead and The Woman With The Beard that looked like a man went across the valley to shave him. She'd get no browner today because she'd have to stay inside and talk to the women that came to talk about her father. 'But even in the days after the stir I won't be able to go down to talk to her,' he said to himself as he lay down for his day's sleep on the straw. He thought he heard a woman crying but it turned out to be the wind screeving across the sharp edge of the chimney-board.

Crying for sure wakened him; crying from the dark. A warm wind under the door was rattling the sticks. Tonight all night the valley would be lively with the corpse. He roasted spuds and went outside to eat them and watch the shadows. He was just sitting down to eat them when he looked down into the valley.

'Christ, God forgive me, what do they think they're at,' he said, throwing the spuds on the rock and jumping down through the whins, whimpering, falling over stones, heading for the hole in the lights. Whins scratched his face and arms. At the bottom of the mountain he bent low so as not to be seen by the lights of the houses. A dog ran after him on the edge of the valley. It started to bark and he caught it and held it under his arm with his hand around its mouth, running the slipe-track up the middle of the valley. 'They can't,' he said. Panting like the dog and tired, he came to the belly-button. It was all right. The candle-stands were still there, last night's drippings on the rocks like what pigeons would do. He let the dog go and threw a stone after it and sat beside a fresh bunch of dandelions hiding under the rock from the moon.

'As long as the stands are there the candles'll come back.'' One candle less; no candle could save The Brown Girl's father once he got the pipe knocked out of his mouth.

He had to listen to things because he was afraid to go back across the valley. Shadows were going between lights and stones were kicking on paths up to houses; people coming from all over the valley to cry in The Brown Girl's house. He listened to bits of talk that people said: 'She's bad this time. She should cry more.' 'Sometimes I waken at night and say something to my man, forgetting that he's not there.' One time, when the door was opened and the crying got louder, he thought he heard her voice singing under the crying. 'Why should she be singing?' The Cripple In The Wheelbarrow was wheeled into the house. But he was no crack, The Cripple; he wasn't the one to make her stop singing.

All night she didn't come out; not even to throw water onto the grass. People went home to houses to put out their candles and some of them laughed at their own talk when they were in the far side of the valley. The Cripple was wheeled down the slipe-track. 'When they're all gone I'll be the only man left for her,' he said to the boy wheeling him. 'I don't know whether I want to be.' Art said to himself: 'Somebody must have told The Cripple that he was a man.'

The moon went round the rock and the shadow pulled back from the dandelions. They looked up at him like small faces. One by one he pulled them and stuck them to the rock with their own white sap.

'She'll see them when she comes out with her candle and she'll know that someone left them for her.' Going home he saw that the first blossoms were coming on the potato-stalks of The Cobbler's land. At home he cut the second deep notch on his days.

He slept so well that the only bit of the funeral he saw was the long bent line of women following the slipe over the back of the mountain. He tried to pick out The Brown Girl but, with so many in black, she could have been any of them. When they left there was nobody lying talking in the potato-stalks; the houses sat still with dead smoke from some of them. None from The Brown Girl's house where the man's boots were. And his jacket and clothes. 'They'll remind her of him and help her to be lonely. I'll have to take them away from her.' In spite of nobody being in the valley he went round the top of the mountain and down the long way to come at her house from the back.

'An ordinary enough house,' he said inside, a little disappointed. Except for the bloody shirt in the tub of water under the table you'd never think it was famous all over the valley. The boots were beside the tub and he tied them round his neck. An ordinary enough house with tins not washed and the dirt of the people that left. He waved a board at the fire; it lit up and he warmed himself. 'Even the bedroom's ordinary,' he said when he opened the door. Apart from the bed for the dead, up from the floor on a kind of stand, and the dead man's jacket on the wall. He tried on the jacket and it looked well on him. 'Where's the one he wore home?' He looked round the walls. Nothing on them but women's coats on pegs. On the straw mattress on the floor there were piles of coats and clothes, the corpse's woman's skirt where she changed into her good one before she went to the funeral. On the edge of the heap, down near the straw of the mattress he saw a scorched jacket that The Cobbler used to wear and coming out from under the side of it was a bit of the bloody jacket with holes. He was just reaching for it when he saw her hair.

That was the only bit of her that came out from under the pile of clothes. Was her hair. A raggedy end of the straw. It came out alongside the bloody jacket from under the scorched one, the very end of it falling down in the dust of the floor. 'She must be under the heap.' But he couldn't see her and if he pulled back The Cobbler's jacket she might waken. He sat on the floor thinking. If he did it quick. . . He pulled it back, jumped into the dead man's bed and pulled the white clothes over his head.

There was no move. He looked out from under the sheet. Not a move out of her, but he couldn't see her because the pile of clothes came between him and her. He tipped out of the bed and crawled along the floor. Easy. So the boots swinging from his neck wouldn't hop off each other. Over the top of the pile he saw her face. Dribbly hair along the side of it and the light from the window in the brown. Closed eyes with marks going out from them, and the collar of the bloody jacket in her open mouth. One of her hands was in the pocket under her head and the other held its collar at her mouth.

'Are you dead?' he whispered.

Her eyes moved under the lids and her lips tightened round a chip of caked blood on her father's collar. The apple moved in her neck. On the side of it there was something alive pumping in and out like the ticking of a clock. For a minute it stopped and he sweated, watching it. It started again, faster, and she took a big breath that frightened him. If she was alive why didn't she go to the funeral?

'I didn't go either,' he whispered.

He raised his head higher over the heap. That thing there was the place where her neck ended and she began; the place where the strings in her neck thickened out towards her shoulders. Sure she wasn't going to move, he went closer to see where the sun didn't get at. The brown was the shape of the fork of a tree and, around it, the rest was as white as the middle of winter. A bit over on the white there was another thing ticking between two bones. The white was bluer there with a drop of sweat on it, shining with the ticking. Around it there were lighter marks like the rings in the lake that he put his feet in. He was so near to her that when he put out his hand he could feel the dew of her breathing on it.

'The lonesomeness is going to kill her unless she can talk to someone sensibler than The Cripple.'

At the edge of the rings on the white there was a small bud near the point of her shoulder with a hair growing out of it. One curly hair. He looked at it, feeling sorry for her. It threw a thin shadow on the white that moved when she breathed, like a whin's shadow if it was windy in winter. He took his breathing from the beating of her dew on his hand and the two of them breathed out together as the hair shook on the bud. Like this he felt like The Cobbler That Had Time To Talk; he was a bit of her and she was a bit of him. People got married for this and the Yoemen took it away from her. She was right not to go to her father's funeral when he wouldn't fight when The Cobbler was killed and still went to fight for the heap of stones that the wind blew into the day that The Cobbler was buried.

One time when he was breathing out he said 'I told Father Murphy that, the day he came for the men. I said "I'm not going when yous wouldn't fight for The Cobbler That Had Time To Talk" but the horse took him away before he had time to listen to me.' Her mouth whistled a little when the hair moved. The flake of blood on the jacket got damp and melted into her, and under The Cobbler's jacket she went up and down, in and out.

'I don't agree with dying either,' he said. He lay on the floor beside the straw. There he could see the armpit of the hand that was in the dead man's pocket. He found the ringlet of her hair to blow. It curled up at the end, moved and twisted, and covered itself with the dust of the floor. A tail of The Cobbler's jacket fell over his feet and the burned cloth broke around his toe.

'Don't die,' he said. 'I'll tell the women why I never went to the fighting and then I'll be able to come down and talk to you and keep you from being lonesome.'

The night came on, darkening the room. The whole house seemed to close in on the side of her face and, in a while, she was a shadow between him and the window. Lying there, helping her to breathe, he thought he knew why God put him into the valley.

Dark came down more. Potatoes fell from his pockets onto the floor and she never moved except for the up and down of herself or a bigger breath that frightened him. The boots were sticking in his back but he didn't touch them till the moon, coming in the window, lit her face again. It looked fresher in the moon; no dirt from rubbed sweat. He sat up, wondering how to get her father's bloody jacket away from her.

'Couldn't do it without wakening her.'

He put the father's good jacket on over the boots on his neck and he pulled away The Cobbler's jacket so slow that she never moved.

'Some of these days I'll tell the women,' he said before he went out the door with one jacket on him and the other in his hand.

Outside he remembered and went back to lift the potatoes from the floor.

There were no lights on in the valley. An odd dog was barking at the high smoke from The Brown Girl's house. He didn't have to run and there were potatoes that might squash in his pockets. So he walked. Going up the middle of the valley with the dead man's jacket keeping him warm he thought that he was just like an ordinary man going home from a céilí in a neighbour's house. He hung the dead man's jacket on a nail, but when he tried to hang up The Cobbler's it kept breaking on the nail and it fell in pieces on the floor. The voices came back to the valley. There was more praying at the button-rock but no crying. The candles were left lit on the rock and one by one the lights went out in the houses.

He spent the night at the candles, reasoning with himself: 'I have to tell them before the rest of the corpses come or they'd kill me for not being one of them.' But, even with doing that, the women might shun him and not let him listen to them talking. 'I'll tell them it was because of The Cobbler I stayed and even when I'm the only man in the valley they'll have to like me.' But what if they didn't believe him? He danced his toes in and out of the shadow of the rock and, when that didn't stop him thinking about it all, he went through the names of the men with the candles. With every candlestick he tried to make a picture in his head of the man it belonged to and, to keep from thinking, he tried to imagine them where they were now. His mind was taken up. Well on in the night the wind rose. It came from the direction of the lake with the fish and the burned chapel where The Cobbler was buried. Two weak candles tried to fight it for a while but a strong blast came and Art held his breath as he watched them. They fought as long as they could and then their flames lay down on the tallow and they died. For a while he watched them, thinking, and then he blew them all out and ran, frightened, along the slipe-track, through the whins, and he lay panting on the straw.

'Now they'll know I'm here,' he said, 'if they don't blame it on the wind.'

In the morning, after smoke came in the houses, they came out and gathered around the rock, talking. He thought maybe one woman might have looked up at his house, but none of the rest of them did, and they all knelt down and prayed. 'They must blame it on God,' he said. The smoke was in The Brown Girl's chimney but neither she nor her mother came out.

The wind blew for a few days from the valley with the lake. Every night he named the candles as they went out. He got to know the night so well that he could blow out the last few and make it to his house just as the lock of sky over the corner of his house was starting to get bright. Every morning the women came with no Brown Girl and prayed. Then one night came with no wind from any valley; the same night as the light stayed on in The Brown Girl's house and shadows ran past the window. The mother came out and locked the door from the outside and ran across the valley to a neighbour. The neighbour came back with her and stayed most of the night.

'She must be bad,' Art said. 'But with no wind the women'll know it's me.'

That night the pictures of the men got clearer; he saw them walking between the smoke of fires — men that winked and slapped each other on the chest; and there was music from beyond where the men were sharpening their pikes. One of them began to talk to him and he answered back. 'It'd be like killing them,' Art said. He sweated at the rock with his mouth close to the candles wishing he could blow. The woman came out of the house, the door closed too quickly, and she went back across the valley. He spent the night with the candles and the lit house. The cock crowed for the morning and he wrapped the dead man's jacket around his face and went home crying across the valley.

'And the worst of it is that this was a night with no wind. If they hadn't got clearer I'd have been able to blow them out and the women would know for sure.'

Mist got thick on the nights in the valley and he sweated and didn't sleep in the day. The light stayed on in The Brown Girl's house and the men got clearer. Some of them talked to him and winked at him and one of them laughed at him. Sometimes they borrowed his pike to kill someone but they always gave it back to him sharper than he had given it to them. Their smoke mixed with the mist. As if to tease his trouble, The Cripple In The Wheelbarrow was wheeled one night through the mist and in the door. He heard him laughing inside and singing a song that no one with an ear could listen to. Going past the rock near morning he said to the boy wheeling him 'she's brightening. To-morrow night you'll have to come again and wheel me up.'

The notches moved down Art's stick. When they came to a wood-knot The Cripple said to the boy 'Seeing how she's coming on makes you feel useful. It nearly makes up for the men being away.'

Art said 'The poor fella; coddin' himself; I'd rather be dead than be him.'

Soon after that, the light went out in The Brown Girl's house as if someone was going to sleep. Art left the candles to themselves, wrapped the dead man's jacket tightly around him and went home to put on the stolen boots. He ran in them up the top of the mountain where he and the moon could look down on the valley's mist. They sank on mountain ground, slithered on rocks, went sideways away from his feet. They ran, carrying him, after his lambs, woolly and afraid, running away from him cheering. 'Baa Baa.' He shouted Ba Ba after them, tripping on stones falling after them. The boots sank in the mud of a drying spring; he loosed the laces and tramped them into the ground, jumping and cheering and singing. He took off his jacket and jumped it in after them, ran over the ground with moss pricking up between his toes, and rolled, cheering, head over heels, down the shiny rocks of a dried stream-bed. The rocks hammered his feet and jaggy rocks along the side cut his bare shoulders, his head rolled in the after-slime; he sank into the wet mud of a catch-hole and, tired and sweating, curled up in it and lay there.

It was that night that he learned the place of

things and what was important and what wasn't. 'I'm only a man,' he said as he lay curled in the catch-hole. 'I can't change them and maybe they'll never like me anyway.' Some day he would open his door and take off the shutters when the women were working in the valley. He'd light a fire and they'd look up and they'd see the smoke curling out of the chimney and falling down on the thatch so thick that it would blacken the whole roof and, when it would be falling to the eaves, a hill-wind would catch it and blow it high and straight into the sky. The women would see him when they looked up and he would wave to them and on his way across the valley to take away The Brown Girl's loneliness he'd stop with them and explain to them why he didn't die and he'd promise them that when all the corpses came back he'd go down and help them with their work. That was the way to be; to put things where they were and not be annoying yourself about things that might never come about or that you couldn't help. He felt that night that he knew something that nobody ever knew; that to decide things was the thing to do. He spread the mud of the catch-hole over him and he danced home in his suit of clay. The next night, when he was with the candles, the news was carried into the valley that The Rising was won.

The horse came down the twirly stones in the dark. Carrying something, he knew, when the step got heavy and slow on the steep fall. It checked and stumbled and a voice said something to it, talking it down the fall. Someone alive. At the last ridge before the valley he shouted 'Anybody there?' and his voice came back from Art's side of the valley. The hooves stopped and started again and, coming down the last slope, the rider moaned. Art crept closer to the rock where he wouldn't be seen. Now and again coming across the level ground he shouted and moaned. At the edge of the light the hooves staggered a little, stopped again, and then it made its last push into the light.

He stood there with his big white knees and a bone growing out of the side of them, mud on his feet and fetlocks and all shining with sweat. Tired but looking strong, his long strong face not bending to look at the grass; he stood as high as the day he carried the last corpse. His stomach was going in and out, all white except for the blood that ran down from the big stranger that carried the dead. He made a farting sound through the bit; the stranger lay back on the reins, and he took a few steps closer to the light. Art tightened himself in to where he could see the horse under a hanging bit of the belly-button.

People started to come, a little afraid, across the valley. The sound of their voices came nearer, changing to whispers when they came close. Skirts beat legs. Dead quiet. They passed close to Art.

'There's only himself', someone whispered, glad. 'Only himself and nobody dead.'

'Then what took him back to the valley?'

The horse. Art saw it through the opening under the rock. Through the legs of the people, gathering, whispering. Nobody noticed the blood that ran out of the man. When most were gathered, they all went quiet and the man began to talk:

'It's as good as won,' he said. 'We beat them at —' he mentioned names like towns. Gorey was a town.

'And the men are safe?'

'On Vinegar Hill, most of them.'

'They should be home soon then?'

'The English are going to attack. After that they'll be home.'

As they started to cheer and talk to each other, Art had the best view of the foot starting to slide round the horse's belly. It moved, first a span along the bellyband, slower over the buckle, and then the man fell into a gap in the feet. When he hit the ground he tried to pull himself up by the reins; the cheering stopped. The horse looked down at him.

The Woman With The Beard went down to examine him and said he was dead.

'Bring him to the dead-bed. I'll go and get my shaving things and I'll tell the crying women to come.'

In The Brown Girl's house the bed for the dead was, they said. The women carried him between them into the dark, into the shadow of the window, and they shouted into the house that there was a man there that said The Rising was won.

The Brown Girl's mother came to the door with a candle that showed the crowd looking at the man with screwed-up faces as if something was hurting them. She held it over her head and looked under it.

'Is he dead?'

'He's just gone.'

'The bed's made and ready.'

The crowd moved like a whirlpool when they started to carry him in, and all of a sudden they stopped and went quiet. People moved round the edge. They were quiet because The Brown Girl came to the door.

She came out, running her fingers along the wall, white and all hollows and her hair wild. She propped her head against the jamb, looking sideways at the corpse. Very low she started to talk to it.

'Don't come in here,' she said. 'They'll only take the clothes off you and steal your boots.'

When she bent her head down, looking the other way, finished talking, the women with the corpse whispered to each other and started to move towards the door. She looked at them coming and let a scream and ran, crying like a kicked dog, across the valley.

'Jesus, Mary and sweet Saint Joseph, catch her.'

They caught her before she got to the end of the light and dragged her, kicking and screaming, into the house. Nobody moved till they did something with her to stop her shouting.

'By the Holy Jaysus,' Art said, 'she's mad.'

When she stopped, the women started to move the corpse to the door. His head was swinging and a young girl from the far side of the valley lifted it with her hands and held it against her stomach. She bent, and her hair trailed his face as she closed his eyes. Before the crowd tightened around the door he saw the horseman in the light of a high candle, lying back in the valley between the women's breasts.

The crying women started up inside and people came from all over the valley even though he was a stranger. The Cripple went home early.

'The men'll be coming back any day now and the women'll be cheering them and looking at them,' he said to the boy. He laughed none going down the valley. To spite The Cripple, Art said to himself 'I'm glad they won.'

He took out his pike and gathered stones around his feet with its blade as he sat on the rock in front of his house listening to things wakening. Clicking things wakened first inside the thatch and the sun came up as bright as a good day. It was well over the chimney when he trailed his pike down the rocks into the valley where people were. They looked at him crossing the valley and children came to windows. The Cripple In The Wheelbarrow crawled on his arms to the door and laughed.

'Hello Art,' he shouted, laughing.

'He thinks he can talk to me,' Art said to himself.

When he came to the door of The Brown Girl's house the crying stopped and women put their heads around doors and the edges of walls. Her mother came to the door, sizing him up with her face.

'How is she?' he said.

'Who?'

'Your lassie. I wanted to ask about her and how she took the dying.'

She looked at him and the women were quiet.

'She took it as well as anybody would take it.'

He twisted on his heel and turned away from her. He said "And the man's dead for sure and Father Murphy's not because the horse never brought him.'

'Yes.'

'That's what you find when you're winning; there's less dies. It's always handy when people don't die."

'Why are you quiet?' she said in to the women.

62

The women started crying again. She moved from the door and came closer to Art and she looked straight at him, a big line-faced woman. 'Poor Art,' she said, and her eyes filled with tears.

He looked at her, not sure what she meant, and he moved away from her towards where the horse was tethered to a hook in the gable.

'I'd better get back to Vinegar Hill,' he said, 'Father Murphy sent me for this.'

He took the horse to a stone and got up on it.

'Don't go,' she said, starting to cry out loud. 'Whoever blew out the candles we don't hold it against them.'

'The men'll be waiting for me,' he said. 'It's a bare place — Vinegar Hill; nothing on it only the Irish on the top and the English at the bottom.'

She went down on her knees and started to pray. He pulled the reins and the high horse went across the valley. Women came from houses to watch him go and he was glad he didn't go the first day when none of them noticed him. Some of them cried and knelt and the girl that held the horseman's head came out into the middle of the valley to look at him. She had long hair down to her waist and she was brown from the sun. They were all there when he sank into the valley with the lake.

He stopped beside the lake at the rock he died on, gave the horse a drink and tied it to the bushes. From the bushes he cut forty small sticks and tied them in a bundle to the saddle of his horse. He took another stick and, with his pike, started to cut notches in it that would show to the day how long he lived.

'I'll always ask a man in some valley how to get to Vinegar Hill.'

The sun was high and the fish were there. His feet sank in the water and made rings.

Still Life

It was the autumn of the early snow that Corr noticed that Ned was failing. The snow came that year when farmers were bringing in digger-wheels to be mended and horses were being shod for the harder ground; it stayed till the farmers cursed it away and when it went they hoked the potatoes from the clotted clay it left behind. On the day of the thaw a farmer found the carcass of a sheep in a hill-hollow and he gave Ned fifty pence to bury it. He promised him a day gathering spuds but Ned said it was late in the year and went in to spend the rest of the day leaning against the forge-door while Corr worked. It was that day that Corr noticed the puce berries under Ned's eyes and the ochre right-angle of his cheek. 'You're done, Ned,' he said to himself. His own woman's face had looked the same before she died. He told Ned stories about women that evening and when the dry grass on top of the yard wall faded into the dark of the sky they went up the yard together and stood for a while in the entry.

'You're a lucky man never got married, Ned,' Corr said. 'You might have ended up like your man across the street. That's what the marrying did for him.'

They huddled against the walls of the entry, looking at the house across the street. It was back a few feet from the line of houses and stones were peeping like eyes through white-washed plaster under the upstairs windows. There was a slate poised on the gutter ready to fall in the next wind, and a smoke-wisp was probing a crack in the swollen chimney.

'That's what the marrying did for him,' Corr said again. 'I'd say it's the head.'

'Women'd put anyone mad,' Ned said with some satisfaction, and after a while they parted because they lived at opposite ends of the town.

'I'd better do something about Ned,' Corr thought on his way home, and he tussled with the problem till he went to sleep.

The farmers got their spuds dug and carted them into the town before the next snow came and some mornings when Ned was kicking the frost from the forge door someone might offer him a day gathering. If it was after eleven he went, but if the day was windy or cold he stayed at the door-post looking up the yard, rubbing himself against the inside of his overcoat or kicking the numbness from his toes on the ground. One morning Corr was straightening an iron bar on the anvil when Ned said, 'I'm fifty today,' and Corr said, 'If you had have gone to England you might only be forty,' and they rattled the marbles of their laughter against the back-walls of the town. The snow was brown on the street on Christmas Eve and in the entry Corr gave Ned ten pence and wished him a happy Christmas. Big-wigging with a farmer in the pub afterwards, Corr said he thought it would be Ned's last Christmas. 'It's the women that's wrong with him,' said Corr. 'Never having had it is going to kill him.' And the farmer said that devil the like of such a useless man ever he had working for him.

'What about your man across the street?' Corr asked.

'Laziness,' said the farmer. 'Nothing a bit of work wouldn't cure.'

'A bad buck,' said Corr, but he was thinking it wouldn't do Ned much good if he knew that. 'The way I look at it,' said Corr to the farmer after a while, 'if Ned's mind could be set easy about what he missed — ' but he didn't finish what he was going to say because the farmer was turned away talking to a man who had bought him a drink.

One morning in the new year Corr was frying an egg on the sock of a plough when Ned hunched down the yard, his fox-coloured coat sanding the top of his wellingtons.

'She's cool, oho, is right, cool.'

Corr turned the egg with the tongs before he said: 'Your man across the street: they say it's creeping paralysis but you never heard of a man taking it so quick. How he walks to the door if he has it I don't know, but he was seen at six this morning standing in the door in his nightshirt.'

'At six, oho, in his nightshirt.'

'Damn that wind,' said Corr as it hammered loose zinc against the roof. 'It'll knock the place down.' And then he said, 'No, I'd say the head's goin'.'

'Terrible, terrible.'

Corr said: 'When the head goes you may look out,' but instead of laughing Ned said, 'Terrible' again, more to himself than to Corr.

'I must fix that buckin' zinc,' said Corr, and when the zinc stopped rattling he said, 'There's nearly only one thing that puts the head goin' and mebbe the two of us knows what it is,' but whatever Ned said was low and nervous and was hustled away by the wind.

'If a body could make up a story for Ned or something,' Corr said to the farmer that night in the pub. 'It's something like that he wants. I wouldn't be much good at the like of that but if someone could take him in hands he could live to seventy.'

'Devil the likes of him ever I saw,' said the farmer. 'Took him half a day to bury a sheep. And I had to pay him to the last ha'penny.'

'If you paid him anything at all you paid him to the last ha'penny,' said Corr.

When he left the pub that night Corr stayed a while looking across at the house. He thought about going down to Ned's house for a while but he could think about nothing new to tell him so he pointed himself home into the wind.

The east wind blew through the first week in January and their talk dripped through the mornings. Sometimes when a magpie landed on a gate or on the grassy wall-top Ned threw a stone at it. An odd time there was a black cloud at the bottom of the town when the postman was whistling past the entry and sometimes a car backfired in the street and that week two people changed the curtains on their back windows. Around dinner-time on those days Ned used to say he had things to do and, going up the yard, he used to stop now and again to kick the dead horns of grass that grew through the stones. It was watching him one of those days that Corr thought, 'I'll have to get a story soon.'

When Ned left, Corr used to fry his dinner on the sock of the plough and all that week a slow sun came over the dry roofs in the afternoons and hung from the cobwebs on top of the door-frame. That week, too, the dust was busy around the anvil where Corr was making harrow-pins for the spring. In the steel light around the amber glow of the fire he used to think sometimes, mostly about Ned and his problem, and he used to get angry with himself for not being able to come to grips with it. One of those nights his wife came back to him in his sleep and she was crying, and from that night on Corr worried even more about Ned. He watched the house across the street for an answer and the day the slate fell from the gutter he saw the outline of the woman between the windows of the downstairs room. She had her hands raised over her head combing her hair and, as he watched, Corr thought he saw her breasts shaking up and down with the movement of her arms. 'She has nothing on,' he thought. He felt an old tension in the middle of his stomach and a darkness crossing his mind and he wanted to close his eyes but, for Ned's sake, he watched, grasping at a drowning thought and whispering to himself a story that was addling his brain: 'She was — he ran after her or something and she — she wouldn't have it and she ran — away.' She tossed her hair on her shoulders and her breasts shuddered — 'and he shouted — and she wouldn't listen — but ran away,' and he turned away and churned down the yard to worry the dead ashes of the fire with a harrow-pin.

'Any word of your man across the street?' said Ned the next morning.

'Last night at twelve he was heard roarin'. About half eleven, I think, she ran across the kitchen floor with nothing on and there was nothing else till twelve when he roared. But he wasn't running across the floor after her when he roared and I don't know whether he was running after her at half eleven either.'

'It's an odd thing that,' said Ned.

'Do you mind ould Gillespie? He was heard roarin' too and after that he started going down the hill. The next thing for your man will be the Mental,' and he heard Ned drawing in his breath.

'I suppose she'd put him wild at night like that,' Ned said. 'Some people's unfortunate that way.'

'Now there was my woman, God be good to her, and she was never like that. Not even after the wee fella came.'

'She was a good woman all right — not like the one across the street.'

'I was often sorry about not being with her when she died and about the wee fella going to England but there was nothing I could do about it.'

'Nothin' at all,' said Ned. 'How could you do anything about that. You can't keep people from dying.'

A wing of burned paper skipped the black furrows of the rafters and the wind curled dust into Corr's eyes. He closed them and wiped the dust from their corners with the tail of his black fair-isle pullover. There were amber trapezoids rimmed with light inside his eyelids, breaking up and dissolving into the tears that were tracking the dust of his cheeks.

'You'd think I was crying for her,' he said to Ned.

'You can't keep people from dying.'

'Last night there was a dog crying and it wakened me and I thought I heard her complaining again and asking me to do something for her. I only half-slept the rest of the night.'

'You have a lot to be thankful for. It'd be worse if you were like your man across the street.'

Corr said: 'You're a lucky man, Ned.'

They talked a long time that day about the man across the street and, going up the yard that night, Corr thought Ned was walking straighter and that he wasn't sinking so deeply into his feet. If he could make him last till spring, Corr thought, he'd be won.

Corr spent only a while looking at the house across the street that evening and he went home early. Before he went to bed he warmed a big stone in the open fire, wrapped a cloth around it and left it in the wee fella's bed to keep it warm in case he ever came back. He lay on the feather mattress he bought the week he was married and, when the fire slowed, the darkness came down on him like sleep. Out of the darkness the light of a summer's day came around him and the woman across the street was younger then. He was looking at her from behind a tree-stump as she came out of the flaxhole, the water dripping from her naked body, and his throat was dry because she was twirling with arms outspread and her face up to the sun. He pressed himself closer to the stump of the tree and the rain came down on the stump and watered the hair on the leaves.

His own woman came back to him that night too, and in the darkest part of the night he awoke thinking that if Ned knew what he was trying to do for him it would be no good, and the thought prodded the rest of his sleep. Once he sat up in bed to think it out but fell asleep with his head balanced on the brass bar of the bedhead. The wind came through the wide space under the door and rustled the tail of the blanket on the floor.

There was a funeral of a widower in the town the next day and after they came from it Ned said: 'The carpenter was saying to me about the fella across the street —'

'She's a tacklin', I tell you; always was. Do you mind Hagan's flaxhole?'

'Near the road?'

'She was in it one day, one of them summers long ago and not a stitch on her. I was passing on the bicycle and she jumped out and ran after me. A terrible thing for a young fella of twenty eight or nine to see and she was nearly a grown woman. I was lucky I got away from her without landing myself in trouble. It's because of that day and things like that that I know more about it than the carpenter.'

'I mind Hagan's flaxhole. It used to go dry in warm summers.'

'God, that wind'll tear the place down. What did you say?'

'It used to go dry in summer.'

'This must have been after a spell of rain.'

For a while Corr said nothing and went on with his work. He couldn't understand why Ned was so contrary about it; if he wasn't going to believe him, Corr didn't see why he should be bothered about him. But that was the way with people: the more you did for them. . . . Ned was screwing the hinge into the doorpost with his thumbnail and rumbling at the cold. If he'd go and work it'd keep his mind off that thing. If he had worked when he was young he'd have been able to keep a woman and he wouldn't be the way he was now. Corr was thinking that maybe Ned would be better dead and that he shouldn't be bothered about him when Ned said: 'Your woman wouldn't have been like the one across the street.'

'No,' Corr said through his teeth.

Ned shifted his weight from one foot to the other and back again before he said, 'How could you know she'd die before you came back?'

'Not at all,' said Corr, 'anyone would have done the same thing.'

They thought for a long time, Ned silent by the door looking up the yard and Corr leaning on the anvil, and then Ned said: 'If your man across the street goes to the Mental it'll be because he can't think of anything else only the woman.' He sounded a bit shaky when he said it, as if he were afraid that Corr would say he was wrong.

The night was closing in on the forge fire when Ned slopped up the yard and, by the time Corr was leaving, the frost had greyed the tar on the doorpost. He rummaged into the sooty tool-box for a bag with armholes in it and put it on under his overcoat before he padlocked the door. The town was busy with rusted Hillmans and the cracked concrete of the street was webbed with frost. He stood in the entry facing the smell of evening onions and looking at the house across the street. The blinds were down, but now and again he thought he saw a shadow moving behind them. He crossed the street and walked up and down a few times past the house, eyeing it under his hat, and then he crossed again and paced the shelter of the entry. He kicked a mountain sheep from the entry and after a gypsy had brought her two children down the yard to beat them Ned came along with the smell of porter on his breath.

'You were drinking, Ned.'

'You smell it off me,' said Ned, pleased, and he asked Corr if he'd seen anything on the other side of the street.

'He's done,' said Corr. 'Do you not see that the blinds are down. That's because he doesn't want people to look in at her.'

'It'd be better for you if it was creeping paralysis,' said Ned. Corr didn't know what he meant and thought it must be the drink that was talking.

'You'd better go home, Ned' he said. 'I'm getting a lift out home in a while.'

By the time Ned left there was no one on the street. A tethered newspaper was circling a lamppost and the wind blew chaff across the bridge of the entry. Somewhere down the street a child started to cry and Corr said, 'You'll break your buckin' father's heart some day.' The lights were out in the town, there was no movement in the house across the street and the child was still crying as Corr headed for home.

He had a headache the next day and didn't go into the forge and that night he left the house to walk the twisty roads above the town. He was looking for Hagan's flaxhole because he thought he remembered something about it and he came to a crossroads that he remembered, but he had forgotten where the roads led to. He stood at the crossroads for the rest of the night wondering which way he should go. As he reached home the next morning Ned came to see if he was all right. He halved an egg with Ned and they went into the forge together and Ned stayed with him all day. They didn't talk much, but, once, Corr started telling Ned a story and stopped in the middle of it thinking of something else. Ned didn't press him so Corr never finished it. As they were watching the house from the entry that evening they heard the radio in the pub forecasting snow. They parted about twelve but Corr only went out the road a little bit and came back and sat watching the house for an hour or so. He sat on a board that night because he was too tired to walk up and down and it was a cold night.

The weather forecast was wrong because the snow didn't come but it blew its breath on Corr as he sat there the next few nights. He got a touch of 'flu but put it over him on his feet. But it made him moodier and when Ned used to bring up about the time Corr's wife died he'd say, 'I don't know why you can't think of something else to talk about.' When Ash Wednesday came he got his ashes and went off fries for Lent so that God would send him some answer to Ned's problem but the only sign God sent was a plucking of snow which feathered his hat as he sat on the board that night. He took it to mean that God was against the whole thing and that Ned mightn't last out the winter. Instead of giving in to God he stopped going down to the forge and, all day and most of the night, he watched for the rustle of blinds or the flickering of a shadow until one night the door opened and she came out, hurried down the street and knocked on the door of the post-office.

He hurried into the entry so that she wouldn't see him and angled himself so that with one eye he could see her waiting for the door to be answered. She knocked again and somebody came out, there was a whisper at the door and she was brought inside. In a few minutes she came out again and went back into the house. Corr went back out and rolled his coat-tails under him on the board and he caught a newspaper that was passing in the wind and put it between his back and the wall. He sat tucked like a penknife, rolling back and forth on his buttocks. His feet became numb and his legs began to sleep. He tapped his feet on the ground and screwed his arms into their opposite sleeves like a muffler but he had to take them out again to rub his ears back to feeling. He felt like going home to bed but thought he would be letting Ned down if he did, so he walked up and down till he got tired and had to sit down again. There was a pain gathering in his kidneys and a shiver was tightening his neck but he knew something was going to happen and he fought with sleep till she came and pressed herself on him. She closed his eyes.

He saw clearly the ambulance being opened and people walking up to the door; people from the ambulance. All the windows of the house lit up. It was an altar in a chapel with bright windows behind it and people talking and whispering like prayers inside the house. He heard 'I'm sure he'll be all right' and he wondered how he had come to be down the yard; lying there not able to move. Was he dying on his own the way the wee fella said he would? If he was it would soon be the coffin's time to come and the wife was sure to come with it. The door opened and the procession came slowly out: the gaunt man lying on the coffin-lid, his hair gone white in the last couple of years, a grey blanket over him and he was looking upwards to the window of his bedroom and into the dark eyes of the blind houses. The woman followed with a case, as straight as a rush on a calm day. She bent over the stretcher and kissed him and he raised his arms to her neck and squeezed it and Corr was at Ned's wake telling everybody who wouldn't listen that he could have saved Ned if he had been able to make up the right things but that Ned always said you couldn't keep people from dying. The engine of the hearse started and it moved off and Corr was powerless to follow it. Prostrate in the yard, whimpering from fear or crying for Ned, his teeth chattering with the cold, he thought he heard a foot fall. 'Are you all right,' she said beside him.

He lifted himself slowly to his knees and shook away the slime which anchored his mouth to the ground.

'I thought I saw someone in the entry and came over to see.'

She was standing between him and the light so he could see only the white braid of her dressing-gown and the streaky light in the bun on top of her head. She bent a little and moved sideways to the light and her half-face looked at him, an arrow probing the hollow around the eye.

'You're the blacksmith down the yard, aren't you?'

Corr let his buttocks back on his heels and tried to say something but only a sigh came.

'I should know you,' she said, 'but I don't go out much.'

Corr rubbed the side of his chin because there was something slimy on it.

'I'll get you a cup of tea to warm you,' she said.

'No, I'm going home.'

He wanted to get up but was ashamed of her seeing him pulling himself to his feet. She must have known, because she turned away. He clawed himself up the wall, stood with his back against it and checked with his hand that his fly wasn't open. She waited for his breathing to quieten before she said, 'Would you prefer me to go away?'

Corr grunted and pointed to his hat upside-down on the ground. She lifted it and handed it to him and he let it hang in his hand in front of his crotch. She paused a minute, looking at the open door of the house.

'Did you see my husband going?' Her shoulders sank a little and Corr thought she shivered but then she drew up her shoulders again and straightened her head. 'They wouldn't let me go with him as far as the hospital.' She turned to him and he saw tears in the corners of her eyes.

Corr twisted his hat a little and said, 'It's —' and turned his eyes to the ground.

She whispered, 'You'd better go home,' and her chin began to quiver a little and she turned away. Corr lifted the hat and put it on his head and shifted his feet on the ground.

'I was working too hard lately,' he said.

He watched her shadow crossing the street and he remembered a time before he was married when his own woman was walking in front of him into the light of a dancehall. Her body was held straight and tight, her head bent to the ground, and no silhouette of her body came through the folds around her legs. She looked across the street at him again before she closed the door and he struggled home and went to sleep.

'Any word of your man?' Ned asked the next day when Corr came into the forge.

'Nothing good,' said Corr. 'He went off last night in the middle of the night. Three men marched him out with his hands tied behind his back and him roarin' and screamin' and kickin' that you'd think he'd waken the town and she came after him screamin' and sayin' that she'd be glad to be rid of him. I told you she was a tacklin' and that's no name for her if you saw her last night.'

'So it's the Mental,' said Ned, sucking in his breath.

'The Mental surely. The people will likely say it's creeping paralysis because they're afraid of getting it themselves but it's funny if you can kick and shout like that.'

'So begod he's away,' said Ned.

'A cold bed she must have had last night. She's wide open for either of us now.'

'But me and you'd watch it,' said Ned.

'We'd be far too cute for that,' said Corr, and he started to laugh.

Ned thought for a while and said, a little unsurely,

'You're not taking it as badly as I thought. I'm glad you're not.'

Corr looked at him, trying to make out what he meant but he couldn't, and he couldn't think what he should answer, so he just laughed. Ned started to laugh too and, not to be outdone, Corr laughed louder. Neither of them wanted to be the first to stop so their laughter grew louder and louder, chopping over the lazy morning town with heavy-wived husbands standing in shops looking out at the weather. It might have been their laughter that acted as a summons for the buck goat that came in from the hills that morning — a buff-coloured one that dragged its hair-pods down the street of the town. He stopped to chew the beard of grass that had started to grow in the horse-manure at the entry and when Corr and Ned chased him he crossed the street to look into the earth-patch in front of the house with its white grass nailed down by dead dahlia stalks and a fawn fungus sucking the stones of the rockery. He sniffed at it and nudged himself down the footpath, chewing the grass along the edges, moving slower than the brown papers and, on his way into the graveyard, he stopped to look in the door of the chapel where the eleven Mass was just ending and the women of the town were praying for a milder spring.

Light Signs

The wood-pigeons came into the roof-valleys early that evening when Brigid was coming in with the apples and Brigid told Assumpta about them: 'They're in twos down along where the roofs meet and they look happy,' she said.

'They shouldn't do that,' Assumpta had said, 'because it's long past the mating season.'

She wondered why Brigid had told her the lie and she was still thinking about it now as she talked about the census: 'How they fiddle it I don't know but there's not as many sheep-farmers as there used to be. I'd say it's communists is at the back of the fiddling and look what they did to the priests in China; if we don't watch out . . .'

The light from the fire freckled the walls where the cardinals hung on dusty cords and Brigid put her hand into its heat hesitantly.

'I didn't like to come up to the fire disturbing you,' she said, 'but I was getting cold down at the table.'

She knelt beside the fire, careful with her dressing-gown, and with her hand polished the brass rail of the fender as far as the lion's mouth.

'About the wood-pigeons,' she said, 'I was thinking that maybe they weren't in twos and that I thought they might have been — that I might have been mistaken.'

'I didn't know you told me they were in twos,' Assumpta said, adjusting her feet on the lion's back.

Brigid sidled on her knees closer to the fire. 'What may have happened,' she said, 'was that I knew you'd be happy to think they were happy and that could have been the reason for the mistake.'

'I'd be more worried about the census,' Assumpta said, 'and the way you can't rely on anything nowadays. I mean, to read the paper you'd think the place would soon be flooded with blacks and how would it be when you think of the prevailing south-west wind which brings rain. There's more blacks in Ireland than there are nuns, it says, but we resolved to be happy tonight so there's no point in annoying ourselves about it.'

She lay back in the rocking-chair so that she was looking down on the shining scalp-line that halved the greying top of Brigid's head. 'No,' she said, starting to rock. 'If the party goes well that's all that matters. Why should anything matter but tonight — census or anything?' She sighed and ran her hand down the long leg of her boots. 'I love you for being solicitous, Brigid,' she said, 'but your jig-saw is waiting and you'd better get it finished before the party.'

Brigid touched the air near the flames and sank back on her heels.

'I'm warmer now, thank you, and I'd better get

back to it,' she said. She shrank behind the chair and rose to her feet and Assumpta saw in the mirror that she caressed the apples with her hand before she sat reflected in the polished table.

'You made great work to get the apples, Brigid,' Assumpta said. 'The gardener must be fond of you.'

'We get on well,' Brigid said. 'But he made me promise to prune all the trees before I leave. It's nice work.' She stopped, afraid she mightn't be interesting, and went on 'You cut off the branch above the bud that grows outwards so the tree can't grow inwards and stunt itself; isn't creation wonderful?'

'Wonderful,' Assumpta said. 'So happy flying around.' She saw in the mirror that Brigid looked quickly towards her. 'I'm sorry. I thought you were talking about the wood-pigeons; my memory's not as good as it used to be. Anyway, all that matters is the party.'

'You'd think she'd have come before now,' Joan said from the bed where she was pretending to read.

'I told you; they've all been busy this last few weeks,' Brigid answered.

'I meant tonight,' Joan said.

'Well, you have to understand, Joan,' Assumpta said, trying not to be angry. 'It's not just a matter of walking along the corridor or across the square. A woman in her position has chores to do, things to be attended to. I mean, if she hadn't, she'd be in here every night since we came here, with she and I being old friends and everything.'

Joan lay back on the bed again looking at a page of the book. She hadn't turned a page since she started.

Assumpta said: 'You could try and read, Joan, dear, if the light was on but we agreed that it was pleasanter to spend the last night in the light of the fire. Anyway you're young. Maybe tomorrow you could try and read. There'll be plenty of light on the train and if you get a quiet place at all you might be able to.'

Joan stretched herself on the bed and didn't answer.

'Maybe you'd close the curtains, Joan, while you're on your feet,' Assumpta said.

Joan got up slowly, bent over the book, and walked out of the mirror into the corner of Assumpta's eye. She stood between the firelight and the steamy lights from the square, fluorescent on the mist outside. Absently she lay against the curtain and the book came up to throw a shadow on the table.

'Tell me about the night,' Assumpta said.

'Brigid's better at that,' Joan said.

'But you can see the sundial?'

'Yes,' she said without looking out.

'And you can see Dympna's office through the mist; the light's still on it?'

'Yes.'

'It'll be a while before she comes in, so.'

'Yes.'

'Brigid, did she tell you she'd be early?'

'She didn't know. She thought she might.'

Joan went back to the bed without closing the curtains and Assumpta was so intent on watching her that she didn't notice Brigid fading in on the other side of the chair. She had a cloth and polish in her hand and she began to polish Assumpta's boots without lifting them from the fender.

84

'You startled me,' Assumpta said. 'I thought you were Joan. You must look young, Brigid, when I thought you were Joan.'

She polished them diligently, bobbing up and down, sweating a little in the heat of the fire. Once Assumpta thought she felt Brigid's hand on the outside of the boots and she tapped her knees with her fingers, thinking she might feel the tapping. But there was no change.

'We want them shining for tomorrow,' Brigid was saying. 'Not that I want to remind you of tomorrow but . . .'

'Not at all,' Assumpta said. 'You have the apple trees to prune and you'll have more time when we're gone.'

Brigid was going to explain what she meant but Assumpta began to cough — a light tickling in her throat that must have prickled a nerve. By the time she had stopped, Brigid must have forgotten what she was going to say. Assumpta said there was nothing in the newspaper of all ever she saw, nothing only the census.

Long after the boots were shiny Brigid stayed by them, massaging them gently with a soft cloth. Around the toes especially she fretted because, she said, that's what would be seen. "Maybe you should take them off for tonight and rest your feet for tomorrow,' she said.

'You never know,' Assumpta said. 'Sometime my legs might want to take me somewhere and where would I be going without boots.'

A fly walked across the top of Brigid's head. Assumpta thought at first that it might be a bluebottle but it turned out to be an ordinary housefly out late for the summer. It flew onto the mirror

85

and walked to the gilt frame across Joan's legs. It went into the shadow above the frame and she lost it.

'I hope Dympna likes apples,' Brigid said. 'I had it in mind to ask her, but I wanted it to be a surprise if she comes.'

'Of course she'll come,' Assumpta said. 'And you're worrying again, Brigid. She always liked apples — in the Philippines long ago when there was plenty of bananas she used to long for apples. But that's talking about the past and we don't want to tonight. No, tonight's the first night in the rest of my life.'

And it was; with the fire and the three red dressing-gowns and the smell of apples and the flames breaking on the chandelier; the reflection of the bookcase over Joan's bed reflected in the table reflected in the mirror.

'Not at all,' she said. 'It's not the apples Dympna's coming for — after all we've only got one each; it's for the singing and the celebration and the spirit; that's what we have to offer — the spirit. Wonderful.'

'Brigid smiled at her. 'You're marvellous, Assumpta,' she said.

'They're not much use, legs,' Assumpta said. 'And what would I be doing going anywhere. Not at my age. I've still got my eyes and arms and you can't read the paper with legs. When Dympna comes in I'll just tell her that one day I had them and the next day they wouldn't work; I'm not going to make a big fuss about legs.'

'Brigid gave the boots a final touch and stole quietly away. She walked back into the mirror and into the shine of the table beside the jig-saw.

Her head was low and her hand, Assumpta thought, was unsure on the jig-saw pieces. She kept watching her as she said 'No, I'm like Woody Woodpecker.' She laughed to herself. 'I remember him once and he was running away from something — maybe it was a big dog or a wood-pigeon or something — when he went slap bang into a tree. All crumpled up he was like a melodeon and the little beak sticking out of the leg of his trousers, but he gave himself one shake and off he went again. They don't make them like that any more — films I mean.'

She laughed again, watching Brigid.

'You're not crying, Brigid?' she said.

Brigid drew herself together before she looked into the mirror. Assumpta was wrong because there were no tears in her eyes and she looked happy enough. She smiled at the mirror.

'I'll be lonely for the two of you, but why would I be crying? Crying would spoil everything.'

'I thought you might have been thinking of my legs and when it was quiet I thought I heard you. I didn't want to take a chance that you might be blaming yourself for my legs.'

'I'm grateful for that and I appreciate it.'

'Because there's no one to blame for them. It's just the way the outside of a wheel wears before the middle of it. Do you know, Brigid, that if you put all the squatters in Ireland together it says you could fill fifty convents with them and still have some over.'

'I'm sure you're right that it's not true.'

'Of course it's true but what annoys me most is that somebody must own the houses and why they do it I don't know. It's a bit haywire as far as I can see, but I'm keeping you from your jig-saw.'

'It's not that important,' Brigid said, bending to it; beside the apples the gloss of her unlined face that Assumpta said was a miracle; the lustre of waiting apples imaged in the table.

The lights were going out in the square between the red curtains on the edge of her eye. All the others going to bed like ordinary life outside a hospital. Except that there was no hum of cars or cheering of footballers who won things.

'No,' Assumpta said, proud as granite in the chair. 'We did good work in Africa, the three of us; excellent work no matter what anyone says.'

Brigid clicked a jig-saw piece against her teeth.

'So there's no need for you to be crying, Brigid,' Assumpta said.

'But I haven't cried this week and I'm happy tonight, as you can see.'

'You're right too, because it was, most of all, I think, the love we had for each other that made the work possible.'

'I've always said that. In every report to Dympna that's what I said.'

'Me for you, Brigid; I for Joan and so on. Even, one might say, you — to a certain extent. So why would you be crying.'

'Thank you for worrying, Assumpta.'

She hurried back to the jig-saw.

'That's what makes tonight so happy,' Assumpta said. 'The fact that you don't cry now.'

She rocked and the cardinals danced, dazzle of flame scattering across their countenances. Joan and the bed swung towards the chandelier.

Assumpta laughed.

'Dympna's going to laugh at me when she sees only the two beds; she'll think I'm like a horse. A horse, you know, Joan, is the only animal that sleeps upright.'

Joan's redness moved in the half-light under the books.

'Long ago she used to fool me like that about things; that's why we were so fond of each other and became such firm friends. This fellow you're going back to, Joan, you don't think he'll be changed?'

'That reminds me,' Joan said, 'I'm thinking of what to do because I know I should be packing.'

'He must have been young when you last met because you were very young. I'm sure he's adaptable, though.'

She asked Brigid again is she was crying and went on to talk about their love in Africa which made the work so efficacious.

'That's why,' she said, 'Dympna will want to come to see us; not that I want praise but she'll feel she has to.'

There was a far burst of laughter from the girls in the kitchen and the clanging of big teapots. Getting everything ready for the morning.

The kneeler moved in the chapel upstairs for the last footfall of the night; fatigued feet on the tyre-edging of the stairs and the locking of a door. The door opened into the corridor and the rattling of beads on keys passed the door with sure feet on the linoleum.

'It's more for old time's sake she'll come,' Assumpta said, not elaborating because she had promised them not to talk about old times tonight, but just to enjoy their last night together. She had a song to sing and she'd sing it through even if she coughed, she said to them, because Dympna would understand and wait till she started the tune again.

'She has a lovely voice herself. Dympna has. You know the voice that sings higher than the others at night so that you can pick her out; that's hers. And a fund of songs, I'm sure, because . . .' She stopped herself, realising she was going to think about the past.

She liked this room, she said, and especially the African ornaments on the sideboard. And the throb of conversation in it which she'd miss more than she'd allow herself to.

'You'll have plenty of talk and company,' Brigid said.

'And it's a nice place the other place?'

There were garden seats, Dympna had assured Brigid; one beside the rose-bushes which she'd like and the sun came through the windows of the chapel in the evenings and coloured the seat. She'd find that seat especially restful.

'That's if I want to go there,' Assumpta said. 'Dympna might want to get me a wheelchair and send me back to Africa. I could always sit out in a clearing in the sun and talk to the people; it's important to talk to people.'

She watched to see if Brigid was crying because that often made her cry.

She musn't have heard it because she was busy working at the jig-saw. Darkness was coming over the misted firelight of the window-pane. Joan packed for herself half-heartedly and stood poised on the bed with her hand balancing the book on the corner of the shelf.

90

'It's likely for a joke that Dympna sent me a red dressing-gown that wouldn't go with boots. She was always one for . . .'

The fly came back on to the rich marble of the fireplace and died because it was out too late for the summer.

'The lights are going out, Joan?' Assumpta asked.

'They're all gone out,' Joan said. 'Even the kitchen-girls are in bed.'

'But Dympna's working on in the office; she was always one for . . .'

'I can't see from here,' Joan said.

She sat down on the bed, a maroon blob in the darkness. Brigid rustled fixedly to the window.

'She's finished in the office,' she said. 'The light's in her bedroom.'

'But it's on.'

'Yes. Shining out on the mist.'

'She'll soon be coming so.'

'You can't see the sundial or the grass, the mist's so thick.'

'Joan's right; you're good at describing.'

'There's probably enough light to see it but the mist's thick and the fire's dancing on the glass.'

Paddling of slippers on the carpet as she went back to the jig-saw.

'If we have to be on the road by four in the morning we should be asleep,' Joan said, sighing.

A coal burst and a stem of smoke spurted yellow petals of flame beside the green marble of the surround. Assumpta coughed and Brigid became erect at the jig-saw. She held her breath till Assumpta stopped.

'I hope the cough doesn't come back,' Assumpta said. 'I don't want to have to go through all that

91

again. Especially since the cough went to my legs the last time.'

Joan went to the window while Assumpta said the number of priests had gone down since the last census. But the number of bicycles had increased and that was a hopeful sign. She stood young and awkward in the fold of a curtain and Assumpta thought she would forgive her everything if Joan would like her again. Since they were called home Joan had behaved as if Assumpta had done something on her and she didn't know why. That's what she was thinking when she saw the light go dim on the window side of Joan's face. When she saw it, Assumpta said, trying to hide her anxiety, 'No, there's not as many of them as there used to be. I'd say it's communists is at the back of it.'

Joan turned in the fold of the curtains, listening for the corridor door to open. Brigid, erect till the light went out, was active in the pieces on the table. Assumpta remembered, she said, seeing the sundial for the first time. It was a winter long ago, but they were no better than the winters now because she remembered the sundial thick with frost and a robin flew from it one day on to her window on the other side of the square. It was a room not like this which was warm with oak things and cream walls. She lost Joan between the corner of her eye and the mirror's edge and was startled when she came to her shoulder.

'I'll rock you,' Joan said. 'I'm sorry; I think I was wrong not to have rocked you before.'

She rocked to the creaking of springs and the beating of wood on wood and Assumpta hummed softly to herself as if from contentment. On backward strokes Joan's hair brushed against her face and she loved that. She wondered why Joan changed and she admitted to herself that Dympna's coming would make her totally happy. Brigid and the apples and the cardinals tilted, the fire sank below her knees and the firelight sported in the thick curtain-folds on the mirror's edge.

'I'm moving around, Joan dear,' she said. 'You're accidentally turning me away from the window. Why are you turning me . . .?'

Joan stopped rocking and rested on the back of the chair. 'I'm sorry, Assumpta,' she said, 'I'm really sorry.'

Assumpta sat straight in the chair.

'Close the curtains, Joan dear,' she said. 'The firelight's nicer without all that light from outside. Besides, if Dympna sees our firelight from outside she might come in and it's getting a bit late. I'm not sure I want her now.'

She pulled the curtains and Assumpta told her to turn on the light. When it went on Brigid said she could see the jig-saw much better now but it wasn't as pleasant as the fire. Assumpta's coughing came back and Joan stretched.

She stretched in the top corner of the mirror and her stretching had the clumsy rhythm of grass changing colour in wind; awkward and young and effortless, feeling upwards to the air, it reminded Assumpta of one African spring when the rain came early, and then Brigid began to cry.

Rigid at the table she held its edge firmly in both hands and only the tears of her cheeks and the quivering of her chin betrayed the half-smile on her lips.

'How's the jig-saw, Brigid?' Assumpta said, seeing that Brigid was near to tears.

The crying burst then and with her handker-chief she wiped the table where the tears fell and then the fingers of a hand rushed jerkily among the cardboard pieces.

'We had such a lovely night,' she said then, putting her fingers to her mouth. 'That's why I'm crying.' Sobbing broke through her fingers.

'Beautiful,' Assumpta said. 'With just the three of us and the great love we had for each other. I wouldn't wish it any other way and this cough, when I get good air in the garden seat, will soon go.'

Joan's hands came down to dovetail behind her head. 'I'll be tired for Gerry tomorrow,' she said.

Brigid's sobbing quickened and she held her chin in her arms on the table and she clenched her cheeks with her fingers.

'You cry with great restraint and dignity,' Assumpta said. 'And I admire you for it,' and Joan turned towards Brigid and seemed sur-prised to see her crying again.

'I hope you didn't cry because I stretched,' Joan said. 'I was just loosening because I was tired.'

Brigid could hold herself no longer. Her head fell on the jig-saw and her arms went limp between her knees. 'I always said it was the three of us loved each other,' she said.

There was silence in the room and she held herself without breathing as if listening to them. The wheeze thickened in Assumpta's throat and she coughed. Before it overpowered her she said: 'You were right, Brigid; the three of us did love each other.' The coughing then was harsh and deep in her and, drained in the end, she had to get a handkerchief to wipe her cheeks. She sloped a little while she recovered.

Joan asked if she could give Assumpta her apple and Brigid ruffled her nose in the jig-saw.

'Eat it now,' Joan said to Assumpta. 'It'll help bring your breath back.'

She took a bite and said it was nice. Joan's arm came across the back of the chair, tilting it backwards.

'There's a hole in the fireback,' Joan said, and Assumpta knew from her that she had stopped waiting for Dympna to come. 'That hole wasn't there when we came; we've been putting on too much coal.'

The dressing-gowns reddened the marble.

'There definitely must have been more sheep farmers,' Assumpta said, 'because I remember them driving in the roads to the fairs and if you counted them there must have been a thousand. In Cork there was more anyway.'

She let her hand slide from the armrest.

'In the country around Cork, I mean; there was no sheep in the city, of course.'

The wheezing came back and she coughed but it didn't go away. Joan lifted the apple to her mouth and she took a bite. The slow chewing vied with the creaking of boards. When she swallowed, Brigid started to cry again.

'What's annoying me too,' she said through her tears to the jig-saw, 'is that the two of you'll be brought to the town in the same taxi and the taxi will bring Assumpta on and Joan will have a long wait for the train. That's another reason why I'm crying; that and the night we had.'

Joan said: 'There's no reason to cry because Assumpta and I are together again.'

After that Brigid pulled herself up because, Assumpta thought, she was too proud.

'I remember,' Assumpta said, 'the wood-pigeons at home long ago when I was a girl. Are the grey ones house-pigeons or wood-pigeons, I'll never know that.'

She let her chin fall on her breast like a dead woman. Joan rocked her gently and the apple fell from her lap behind the fender.

As she rocked her, Joan talked about the early morning train. The town would be still dark when she got there, she told Assumpta, but she would like the quietness and she could look in the shop windows for clothes she might buy and the station would be open all night for cattle-trains. The way up to the station would be dark and she liked that, too, with the reflections of the station lights in the wet street. The station would be warm and she liked stations and she could buy coffee. Assumpta remembered the stations in Africa that were built around a bell and a water-tank and an old man with a goat and a woman with her face shining in the sun. As Brigid's chair moved Joan said: 'I don't know why the cattle-trains stop; they never seem to pick up anything.'

Brigid was still sobbing as she stood beside the table. 'I'd better pack for you, Assumpta,' she said.

Assumpta's wheezing got worse and the coughing came like laughter. She held the arms of the chair tightly and bent over her legs. Joan tapped her on the shoulder-blades till she got it up and, recovering her breath, Assumpta thanked her. She rested her chin on her collar-bone and hung over the side of the chair, the screech of old gates in her throat.

'The trouble with my teacher,' she managed to say, 'was that he had no lad; that's what made him cross, I think. He had girls all right but I'd say he would have used the cane less if he had a lad.'

Through her wheezing she heard the clicking of a case being opened and the rustle of things being folded, the sound of Brigid's small hands timid on them.

'I should have given you both a present,' Brigid said, 'but I can't think what to give.' The case closed and the chair moved and the jig-saw pieces rustled again. Although uncertain Brigid said 'It's useful work pruning the apple-trees.'

Joan rocked Assumpta again. She drifted into talking about Cork and the time she visited the city. She remembered the trees along the river and going up the Grand Parade with her mother to the Opera House. There were cart-loads of things on the Grand Parade that time and a man with a fox on his shoulder was sitting along the footpath drawing people. She sat watching the people and he drew her and he told her to keep it till she was old but she lost it somewhere — maybe in Africa which she loved as much as Cork. She said things about Africa but she knew they didn't make sense because she was getting tired and it was harder to draw her thoughts together.

Very clearly she said: 'I wish I could lie down; this sleeping sitting up gets harder all the time,' before coughing took her again. Joan stopped rocking while she coughed and when she was finished she rocked her smoothly again. What Assumpta said after that was into her chest and muffled. It was about Africa but the coughing and the effort to breathe made it difficult to make herself understood. Brigid stopped breathing and Assumpta said 'I'm glad you stopped crying, Brigid.' Joan's hand touched the top of Assumpta's head and lifted it to the doily on the chairback. She stopped rocking the chair and went back to her own bed.

'If this doesn't stop,' Assumpta said, 'the heart will give. But it'll be all right tomorrow, Brigid, don't worry about that.'

She talked about bonfires they had and about gathering potatoes on long evenings stretching into November. 'My mother, God rest her, had trouble with her eye. She fell on a shovel-shaft when she was young and it kept falling out and we used to laugh at her. So she only cried with one eye when I left.'

Joan was on her bed looking at the chandelier. Assumpta asked her to turn off the light again; it was too glary on her eyes, she said.

'That's odd,' she said when the light went out. 'I'm after trying to move my left arm and it's as if there was no feeling in it. Maybe it's only sleeping but I hope the coughing's not getting to it.'

The fire was going down. The ashes coated the coals and deep in the heart of the fire there was a stirring of moving things. The lion on the fender gaped at the tongs.

She couldn't see Joan or Brigid too well now that it was darker and when she heard the door opening at the bottom of the corridor she thought it was one of them moving. The footsteps came nearer; soft footsteps with the swishing of skirts and the rattling of beads against keys, hard shoes nasal on the linoleum and the faint tinkling of cups. There was a little drumming of fingers on the door, gentle and private, and footsteps retreating into the empty corridor.

'Brigid,' Assumpta said, 'did you hear that?'

Brigid got up and washed her eyes in the basin before she opened the door. She stood for a minute at the door looking into the corridor.

'As I was saying,' Assumpta said quite strongly, 'I have only happy memories of Dympna.'

Brigid went out and the door closed behind her. Assumpta pulled herself up in the chair, her throat rattling. The whispering in the corridor went on for a long time and the door opened again. Brigid walked around the edge of the mirror with a tray with tea in silver things and tinkling saucers with coloured biscuits. She left them on the table and closed the door.

'That was Dympna,' she said. 'She sent you this.'

She left a saucer in Assumpta's lap and Assumpta took the cup in her right hand.

'Leave the biscuits in my lap when they come,' Assumpta said. 'This left hand's not . . .'

Brigid gave a cup and saucer to Joan and poured tea for both of them. She left a small plate of biscuits in Assumpta's lap and another she left on the bed at Joan's shoulder.

'She didn't come in,' Assumpta said.

'No,' Brigid said. 'She was in her dressing-gown, you see. She was ready for bed.'

She was sitting at the table when she remembered that she had forgotten to give them milk. She
gave it to them and after Assumpta said 'It's
miraculous the way you can make do with one
hand. That's wonderful tea,' they settled down to
eating quietly together. Assumpta couldn't rock so
the cardinals were steady on their dusty cords.

'She said she was all ready to come and see you,'
Brigid said, 'and when our light wasn't on she
thought you had gone to bed early.' She looked
at both of them in turn, 'With having to get.up
early in the morning,' she said. 'And she was just
in bed when she saw our light going on and she
thought we might like tea.'

'That's what took so long in the corridor —
explaining that,' Assumpta said. She coughed
and the mucus came up, allowing her to breathe
easier. 'Thank God she didn't come. I really get
embarrassed by praise, and you have to go on, you
see, praise or no praise. Besides, by not coming she
cleared up things and I know who to forgive.'

Before she finished her tea Brigid poked the fire
so that it would be warm on Assumpta for the
night and she put a rug over her legs. When she went
back to her tea she noticed that the biscuits were
a bit damp. 'It was really wrong of Dympna to do
that. I'll have to speak to her severely about it; it
being your last night and everything.' Sitting at
her tea she kept working on the jig-saw. Fidgeting
of pieces in the house where even the maids had
gone to bed. No ticking from the sundial. They
finished their tea and Brigid collected the cups
and saucers and put them on the tray. She left
the tray outside the door again and went back
to the jig-saw.

'No,' Assumpta said, 'what odds about a hand. According to the census there's more disabled people than geniuses and they seem to be getting on the best.' She lurched back and forth till the chair was rocking of its own will and the strong grey reeds of her hair swung in the halo of the fire-light.

Joan came into the ring-light of the fire. 'I mightn't bother about Gerry,' she said.

'You're young,' Assumpta said. 'That's what you have to recommend you and you'll get on well. If you want to read you can turn on the light.'

She turned it on and pulled the curtains back.

'Tell me about the night, Joan,' Assumpta said.

'You can see the sundial in the light of our window. The mist's gone.'

'Dympna's gone to bed?'

'There's a reflection of our light in her window.'

'You're as good as Brigid at describing.' she started to rock again.

Joan went to the bookcase, ran her fingers along the titles, selected one and, lying on the bed, began to read.

Brigid said: 'Dympna talked to me today about going back to Africa.'

'Well, whatever she said was wise, I'm sure, and the work must go on,' Assumpta said. 'I mean, that's the point of the whole thing.'

'She said India,' Brigid said. 'Africa would have too many memories for me.'

'Of course she's right. It's bad to go back and try to make things as happy as they were before because you can never do that.'

Brigid got up from the table again and went

to the sideboard. She fiddled among the brown dolls and carved men and sticks with painted cracks. She picked out a black man carved from ebony and ran the fingers of her small hands along its grooves. 'I'll give you this, Assumpta, as a memento of me.' She put it in Assumpta's case.

'Take off my boots,' Assumpta said, 'I want to freshen my feet.'

Brigid sat in the fender with her back against the marble. She began to unlace them.

'The thing about Indians is this,' Assumpta said, 'and you'll have to learn to be careful of it: they're tricky; they won't argue with you; they'll agree with you but you never know what they're thinking. That's just information I picked up somewhere that I thought might be useful to you.'

She lay back in the chair, her head on the doily, and the chair began to rock soothingly. She heard the boots coming off her feet and Brigid putting them on the mantelpiece. Brigid lifted the half-apple from behind the fender and brought it back to the table.

'The jig-saw's finished,' she said to Joan in a while.

Assumpta heard it being broken up and the pieces being slid into the box to be ready for the next night, Brigid walking around the room tapping and clicking things against each other and she believed she heard her dusting the cords of the cardinals. An apple rolled under her feet when they were being put back into the bag and it more or less wakened her. She roused herself and shifted in the chair.

'Sometime,' she said, 'I must go back to Cork.

When you get fixed up, Joan, and get a car you can call for me and we can go together. We'll go down by the river, I think; you see young people by the river that you could talk to.'

She settled back into the chair and, though still wheezing a little, her breathing became deeper. The figures hazed in the mirror and her eyes closed on the chandelier where the light broke. A fly buzzed somewhere, she thought, but she knew it must be in her ear and she didn't worry about it. After she heard the clinking of cups leaving the corridor she snored and, still asleep, she heard, sometime in the night, the light going out and Joan and Brigid going, for the last time, to their separate beds.

A Growth Of Some Kind

'It's not a hernia,' the father said, 'it's a growth of some kind.'

He was hunkered down beside a pile of straw, teasing it out for the twister, tugging now and again to feel the strength of the rope between them. He kept his back to the boy. Working away. The rope lengthened and they wrapped it around a corn rick. Then they made another. They worked together till dark, the boy thinking of owning the place, of being independent, maybe even lonely. If it wasn't a hernia he knew what it was but he didn't say anything about it and they went on the hill again the next day.

Cutting rushes to thatch the cornricks, the father swung the scythe as strongly as he had ever done and he talked about the fine tow of hay flourishing through the stubble as if practising for the growth that would come when spring came. All around them was the clatter of balers and mowing-machines and the voices of farmers shouting at each other from hills. The boy waited for him to say more about what the doctor had said and he thought, when they sat down for a while to rest near evening, that he would. But he talked about the gaps in the neighbours' potatoes and poor corn on other fields and he noticed a rabbit that came out from the old fort at the top of the hill and he seemed worried about it.

'Up there was full of them long ago, till I brought in one with myxomatosis,' he said. 'They were lying around swelled and blind for months after it. Dying.'

When they were going home together the boy was still trying to make sense of why the father wasn't crying because he was going to die. The weapons on their shoulders were getting damp from the light drizzle that was beginning. The grass was dampening too and little seeds were sticking to the father's boots. They clung there till the heat of the fire dried them out and loosened them and, by the time they were going to bed, they were scattered near the ashes on the floor. The rain stopped outside and the sky cleared. From the bed where the boy lay he was able to look out the window and, to give himself something else to think about, count the pin-lights in the clusters of stars.

'Are you not sleeping?' the father said.

'No. I can't stop thinking.'

'Neither can I. If we don't get rid of them rabbits before they get a grip we'll never be able to. The myxomatosis will be no good this time.'

They were quiet for a while, each listening for the sound of the other's sleep. Then the father turned in the bed and the boy coughed to let him know he was awake.

'You have no idea of all the holes under that fort,' the father said. 'It's like a small town up there.'

When the boy wakened the next morning the father was already up and cutting copper wire into lengths which he bent and twisted with the pliers to make snares. Before the boy had time to eat anything they were climbing through the sloe-covered blackthorns and into the fort's ring. There were rabbit pills and fresh clay at the ends of the burrows and a track or two through the thick grass. The boy was given a hatchet and told to cut strong stay-sticks which he hammered into the piles of loose clay. The father came after him fastening the ends of the snares around the sticks, saying anything he had to say in a near-whisper as if afraid the rabbits might hear him. It was near dinner-time when they had them set and the boy was hungry. That evening they visited them and twice a day from that on and one day, about a week later, they caught two in two burrows on a ledge of ground. They were like twins, facing each other like delph dogs on a mantelpiece. Their faces were wrinkled up and their eyes closed to slits as if they were smiling. The tightening wire had cut through the fur on their necks and the ground was torn around where they had struggled. They took them home and made soup of them.

'They must struggle a lot,' the boy said when he was carrying them home.

'Surely the devils'll struggle,' the father said.

The balers quietened in the countryside and piles of bales dotted the big fields around them. It was the time of year when it was normal for people to die and funerals passed oftener along the road which could be seen from the house. Mostly they were funerals of old people whom

106

the father said too much feeding had killed. The hearse came over the bridge at the end of their lane, the people walking after it; it went behind a low hill then and the boy could hear the engine straining on the heavier pull up to the crossroads where other cars were waiting. It came out again from behind the hill as it took the last bit of road to the cross and, as if to greet its appearance, the engines of the waiting cars stuttered and started. The boy watched them from the mound of earth behind the back window which faced the road. They all looked the same, some longer than others, some with a louder starting of cars on the crossroads; he noticed that the people behind them always walked with their hands in front of the tops of their legs.

The stalks were dying too as the father began to get slower: nettles were whitening and the high seeded dock-weeds on the mound were hardening and turning grey. In the narrow ridges the potato-stalks had already turned down their heads, some of them had broken in the middle and the top was clayed over again by the spattering of rain on the ground. The father dug them and the boy gathered and all through the slow flattening of clay and the piling of pits they went up to the old fort first thing in the morning to see what the dawn had brought. The snares were always empty and the father became more cheerful as the days passed. The time changed to winter and the evenings came an hour earlier. Towards Christmas they began to go up only once a week just to make sure.

'We got them just in time,' the father said, 'If we had let them get a grip . . .'

The boy could see him failing as Christmas came; he became thinner and he bent like the wick of a candle. His feet toed out when he walked, as if he was less certain of his step, and when he opened his jacket at the fire at night it seemed as if his middle was thickening. It was down there the trouble was, the boy knew; he had begun to rub his hand across it lately; stopping it if he saw the boy watching him, and he belched sometimes sitting up in bed at night. Wind, he said. When the snow came just before Christmas he went out and stood in it as it was falling. It fell on his hat and on his face and it melted and trickled down his neck; he gave it time to gather on his shoulders and on top of things in his open pockets; the wind made it thick against the ribs of his pullover. 'It's only snow,' he said when he came in and the boy told him to be careful with himself.

The snow stopped them from going up to the hill. It was still there when Christmas came and Christmas day brought another fall. They were inside and the heavy flakes were melting down the window-pane. The father brought out a case of stout he had bought when he was in with the doctor and he let the boy drink for the first time. They sat with the case between them, talking, the boy thought, like two men. The day was dark from the snow-clouds and the fire lit up the whole kitchen. There was a bag to the back of the door to keep out the cold.

'This is what I call comfort,' the father said. 'What odds; it's the end of a year and we might as well enjoy ourselves.'

They played cards for a while and then draughts. Near the end of the third game the boy took a long time to make a move. When the father's turn came he was splayed out on the chair fast asleep, his elbow awkwardly on the table beside the chicken-bones. With nobody to talk to, the boy kept drinking on his own. With his drinking the fire became warmer and the face of the man in the chair became more kind. The face of his dying became kinder too; what would his father be except asleep? What would he be, a soul? This kitchen with the light changing on the walls was a place worth being in. Even on your own. You couldn't just rub out things like the snow coming down on the window-pane; or the glittering drops of sweat on the bare stone where the plaster was peeled. You could see how nice it was, even without anybody lying beside chicken-bones. He was on his own now and was making some great sense out of his loneliness. He was able to hold down what he wanted to say to himself or he could let it go; he could cry or be happy or decide to be nothing but being. It was all between the father and him and the game of draughts; after another while, between him and the game of draughts which he could play with himself; that was all it meant.

The father brought a mug of tea down to the bed to waken him. Under the bedclothes he still had his clothes on. A glary light came through the window, blueing the walls of the room. He knew that Christmas was over.

'Is it stopped snowing?' he said.

'It's all fallen,' the father said. 'There's nothing left up there to fall.'

'We had a great day,' the boy said.

'It has to be paid for like any other; the drink's

all gone.'

The empties stayed in the corner. The days warmed up a bit to fool the coldness of the nights. Night and day there was the purring and rooting of cars stuck behind the hill on the sharp chuck up to the cross. Dead weather, the father called it. And prime weather. The snow left the fort first and it was slushy on the hills the day they walked up to it again.

There was a bit of powdery snow under the bushes. Snow with tracks in it. When the father saw it he stopped. His face was flushed. He pulled a piece of branch slowly from a blackthorn and ruffled the snow back over the tracks till they couldn't be seen any more.

'Christ,' he said.

He sat there for a few minutes as if he wasn't strong enough to go any farther. The stub of blackthorn dangled lazily on the snow.

'We're gone,' he said. 'They bucked us.'

At the face of the first burrow they came to there was a thing in the snare. Its head was stuck into the ground and the rest of it was hung across the stay-stick. The fur was peeled off it and thrown back from its neck like a rope; what was left of the flesh was weathered and grey except for the pink mark of fresh teeth under its legs. Its ribs were set like the prongs of a buck-rake and from inside them a trail of things like pink peas had been dragged out. From where the tail had been a trace of green sticky stuff tracked down its side and was seeping back into the burrow and away inside the ribs in a dark hole where the backbone met the shoulder there were big creepers crawling around, only their shine showing when they moved.

'It looks shocking,' the boy said. 'We should have come up even in the snow.'

'Damn them,' the father said. 'Why did they have to come back now?'

He kicked the roots of the bushes, his teeth clenching, his fist banging into his palm, like a mummer doing a Christmas dance.

'We should bury it,' the boy said.

'Bury it? More like we should string it up on a bush to frighten the rest of the friggers.'

He rushed around from burrow to burrow, hardly able to look at the clods of fresh pills, the scraped clay, the paw-marks on the odd patch of snow. The bushes cut him as he ripped around their roots; the knees of his trousers were sopping from creeping on the wet ground. By the time he had gone around them all he was shivering. He came back to the boy, still sitting beside the raw thing at the burrow's mouth.

'We didn't get any more,' he said. 'What are we going to do?'

He bent down with a sudden pain as if somebody had stuck something into him. He held his stomach as he hunkered down, coughing, a trickle running from his mouth onto the fresh clay. There was a kind of stoppage in his breath, a bunged-up feeling about the way he choked back his coughing.

'Is it bad?' the boy said. 'Can I do anything?'

'Them friggin' rabbits,' he said, his voice hoarse and strained. 'You'd think they sensed the wrong time to come back.'

His face was screwed up with anger and pain. He held on to a bush so tightly that it broke in his hand.

'I'll get the doctor if you like,' the boy said.

'No, it's only a wee stab,' he grunted. 'Maybe if we set the nooses smaller they might work; they're likely young ones that can hop in and out through them.'

He seemed to get new ease from finding out what to do.

'Come on.'

He wiped his mouth with a tail of his shirt and they went round the burrows again. He showed the boy how much to tighten each noose and the boy helped him. When they came back to the grey thing again he pulled two sticks and loosened the noose from the flesh. He kicked it on to the slope over the sour water of the moat. It rolled down through the long grass, tumbling over itself the same as the boy, when he was younger, tumbled down the hills. It landed in the moat and the water bubbled. Then the scum on top of the water closed in again.

They didn't get any rabbits though fresh pills peppered the clay and new tracks were beaten through the grass of the fort. They tried different sizes of noose while the farmers around the countryside were venturing new tractors onto the thawed ground.

'It's all right for them, you see,' the father would say. 'They've all bought up new land since the rabbits were here last. Even if they eat an acre or two of theirs it won't make that much difference.'

Day or night he talked about little else. It was hardly after dawn one day when the boy wakened feeling an emptiness in the room. The father wasn't in bed. Worried about him, the boy got up to look for him. He found him in his bare feet sitting on a stone in the street outside, looking up towards the fort. When he heard the boy behind him he just turned around to show that he knew he was there and then turned back to the fort again. That morning he took the gun down from the loft in the kitchen and oiled it. The pin clicked when he pulled the trigger and the bore was still shiny when he showed it to the boy.

'We may have to use it,' he said. 'The only trouble is that cartridges are so dear. The wee beggars are hardly worth it.'

The next day that he went to the doctor he came back with tablets and a box of cartridges and he left them together in the window. They sat there as if he didn't want to use either of them. He still tried the snares, shifting the stay-stick a little, widening or narrowing the ring of the noose. When they went up to the fort in the evenings the rabbits were out in the fort-ring eating the grass and taking the last heat of the sun. Surprised by the father's shout or the clapping of his hands they scurried into the burrows and a startled squeal sometimes told that one of them had been less than careful. The boy never went to the burrow-mouth with the father when he was giving the final chuck to the noose.

It was all chaff against the wind: the grass bared in the ring; new holes cut into the ground and the top-scraw sometimes split along the line of a tunnel. As the hay began to grow on the top hill patches of grass-stubble came around the ends of rabbit-paths and then one day a burrow appeared on the hill itself. That was the day the father began to take the tablets to kill his pain. The same day the weather was brightening and the farmers all around began to plough. They were changing the colour of the countryside, the boy noticed, as he went up the hill holding the box of cartridges for the father. The father tried one shot, but the rabbits scurried away.

'There's a bit of shake coming in my hand,' he said, and he didn't try any more.

The shake was in his hand even sitting at the fire. And his feet twitched sometimes. He went to the doctor oftener and always brought back more wire so that, by the time they began to dig manure into the potato-patches, the fort was a maze of strung wires and grass-covered nooses. The father walked around the fort-ring the way big farmers did when they were lining out sites for piggeries or houses or planting trees. He'd stop and look around thoughtfully, turning quickly to look in the opposite direction, deciding to put a noose here, a strung wire there. Heavy pockets of skin were pulling the lids away from the bottom of his eyes so that they seemed bloodshot and the lines on his face had gone so deep that even when he washed it deep-cut hair-cracks of dust and grime stayed there. Although, as a result of his work, he caught more rabbits, more holes came in the hilltop and the patches bare of hay became bigger.

'Why don't we get the neighbours' dogs?' the boy said.

'The neighbours' dogs are too well fed; they'd let a rabbit run across their feet. Anyway if you can't do a thing yourself . . .' He took down the gun. 'I'm going to have to show you how to use this,' he said. 'It's the only chance now.'

Climbing the hill made him sweat and his

palms were sticky when he was showing the boy how to line up the sights and mind he hadn't his chin in the way when it kicked. They waited till the rabbits came out of the hilltop burrows. One came venturing farther down the hillside than the others and the father whispered that that was the one to get because it was an explorer that would show the rest of them. It was snuggled into itself on the hillside, biting the grass and putting its nose up to sniff the air while it chewed. Its nose was shivering like his father's hand and it seemed to be looking straight at the boy when he fired.

It jerked upwards and began to run towards the burrow.

'Run,' the father shouted.

The rabbit turned as if frightened and confused by the shout. As the boy ran up to it it began to come towards him, joggling up and down as if trying to beat its head off the ground, a mist of live water splashing from the grass behind it. It rolled over and came on. The boy stopped, frightened. It turned again and he saw that one of its forelegs was a bloody mess which shook like a third ear as it ran.

'Get it,' the father said.

'How? How?'

'Jesus Christ,' the father said.

It was skittering through the grass in frantic choppy circles, squealing and whining.

'What will I . . .?'

'Stand on it, kick it, anything.'

He tried to run towards it, but the father passed him. The father tried to trample on it.

'Will I get a stone?' The boy didn't know what

115

to do.

The father tried to throw himself on it to smother its movement. He fell on the ground and went crawling hopelessly after it, trying to beat at it with his hat. The two of them were foozling around through the grass, the father growling and snorting, the high-pitched scream of the rabbit going through the boy's head. The boy made a dash at it, stooping low into its path as it came around the circle. It gave a kind of twist and seemed to jump into his hands. He squeezed it to himself. It was hot and throbbing. Itchy against him. It cried again; its blood on his sleeve. He beat it against the ground, put his foot on it, kicked it with the other foot. It stopped squealing but still he hit it, trampled it with his heel, squashing its head. His boot was red and the blood was squirting to the bottom of his trouser-legs, but still he kicked, grinding it into the ground, frightened by the feel of its fur through his boots, by his own shouting, by the anger with which he was battering the remains of it into the softening ground.

'You have it,' the father said. 'That's enough.'

He beat on till it was raw pulp mixed with clay.

'Now,' the father said.

It was a word which caused him to stop. He looked at what he had done. There was the sound of his own rasping breathing and his father's satisfied hum.

'I got it,' the boy said.

He was overjoyed; a great feeling of power going through him; the same feeling as he had when, years ago it seemed, he used to run to the road to watch big machinery passing and feel the push of the big wheels and the thrust of the spiky things inside its belly. He felt the same push now. He cheered aloud. As was the custom in the country-side somebody else cheered back from some hill. He cheered again and somebody else answered. He lifted the rabbit from his feet and flung it down the field. It fell on a branch in the dividing hedge and hung there. He cheered again; the sound of tractors and bulldozers came back.

He sat beside the father on the wet ground. His breath was still coming in short gasps. The father put his hat back on. Below them were the eight fields and the peeled house that the boy now suddenly looked on as his.

'You see?' the father said. 'You had to do that; you're going to have to be like that. If you're not, the rabbits will walk over you, everything'll walk over you; the neighbours'll have this place and they'll move in bulldozers and dumpers, level out the ditches and this'll be one big ten-acre field with a combine harvester cutting it and the house'll be a byre for cows.'

'That's what it'll not be,' the boy said.

'Look, even if it breaks us we'll get cartridges; it'll be slow, but we'll keep the snares too and the shots might frighten them off their paths into the snares. We'll do for them all in the end. Every one of them.'

He talked a lot as they went home. Everything seemed to be brightening and he seemed to have hope again.

It was a slow slog. After every shot the rabbits stayed in for hours before they ventured out again. Whatever their haste in going back in, they seldom got caught in the snares. Sometimes he missed. The days were short for waiting for them and there were other things to be done: slow digging with a spade in the patches between the rocks that the plough couldn't reach; they set the early potatoes there first because the low fields where the corn would go weren't dry enough to hold up a horse and plough. Standing in the hollow between ridges on a sunny day in early spring the boy was contented that the bare patches were moving no farther down the hill. And happy that, when the days of summer came, longer days with less work to be done, he could stay up there all day till they were all gone. He heard a belching sound from the father as if something was rumbling inside him and he looked around.

His father was down on his hands and knees on the ridge coughing and choking out curds of food like biestings after calving. It trickled out; scraps of potatoes and boiled rabbit and sour water which made him shake his head and shiver. Some of it had gone up his nose, causing his eyes to water, and he was making a blowing, snuffing sound through his nostrils. His back was arched and his legs bent as if the weight of what his stomach was heaving up was too much for them. The choking sound stopped and he bent there, hardly breathing, waiting for more to come. His hat had fallen to the ground and the sun caught the bristly hair at the back of his neck. He looked like a sick greyhound or an old man praying. As he wiped the water from his eyes he saw the boy watching him. He put down his hand and lifted some fine clay and put it over the spew. 'The clay is better than any disinfectant,' he said. Seeing how ashamed of himself the father was, the boy made an excuse to go to the far side

118

of the field. When he came back the father was
sitting again on the ridge, sweat dotting his raked
forehead. 'That damned rabbit,' he said. 'They
won't agree with me inside or outside.' He tried
to laugh.

'Maybe we should go in,' the boy said. 'You're
working too hard.'

'When we have this bit finished we will.'

They went in early that evening and they
tried to spend the time talking, but they had
talked out most things and it was hard to find
anything new.

The father showed him how to plough and
watched him doing it; he advised him not to lift
the plough too soon on the headland or he'd tumble
the horse into the ditch and he showed him how
to lean his weight to turn the plough. From trying
it the boy became strong enough to do it. He
found himself growing; coming level with the
father's eyes. He noticed in the evenings the gaggle
when the bus stopped on the crossroads to let out
the young people from the secondary school and
he heard the screams of the girls as the boys ran
after them behind the hill. He hadn't much time
for them, but he did take time, sometimes when
he was waiting for the rabbits, to watch a girl who
got off a later bus. She'd go down the slope and go
behind the hill and he'd wait till she came out
from behind it and across the bridge. She must
have worked in town, he thought. One day when
she stopped at the bridge to look down into the
river he saw the father on the mound at the back
of the house looking at her too. He was standing
straight and still with a spade in his hand. The sun
was casting the shadow of his hat on to his face,

so that it seemed as if his face wasn't there at all. It was as if there was nothing standing there only his clothes; like a scarecrow with a wire holding up his hat. The boy wondered what he could be thinking.

There came more tablets from the doctor and packets of things. He never showed any of them to the boy, but he guessed that some of them must be to rub on the sores that were coming in the creases of his skin, like the wet oozing line where his neck met his shoulders. When he was going to the doctor the boy helped him onto the cart; he had stopped eating and he was so light that the shafts hardly tilted when he crossed the tailboard. Before he moved off he always told the boy something he should do when he was gone and always when he came back he asked if he had done it. He brought home more cartridges, but he never wanted the boy to go as far as the town with him. It was between him and the doctor, he said; the doctor, he said, thought he was getting on well. Easter came and the Resurrection. He went nowhere. 'No use changing your mind at the last minute. Even if there is somewhere to go I'll not go begging for it.' He stood in the door in the evenings; the grass was growing well and young shoots of potatoes were coming; the corn was abraird. Out of the blue he'd say, 'It's just a matter of time till you get rid of them all' Although the boy knew he was in pain he seemed to be able to keep the pain outside himself so that, even doubled up in a chair with a cold sweat dripping from his forehead he could still talk in a quiet, strong voice about how the land might be improved or how he might try to shoot two rabbits at a time to save cartridges. They talked a lot in the evenings at the fire. The boy liked these times. He put logs on the fire as he had always done and he listened more than he talked. Nights went by like this as if nothing was changing.

But the father was. The vomiting came oftener. The boy got used to the smell of it always in the house or even standing beside the father in the open air. He became able, too, to know from the father's shiftiness when it was coming and he could move away and leave him on his own with it. He might make an excuse to go to the other side of the field or he might go up the hill where he could now shoot a rabbit without any mistake; sometimes he had to kick it or strangle it to finish it off, but he never missed. When he came home from the hill the smell of vomit was always fresh. As the weather became hotter the boy found it harder to sleep. All night the father made noises in his sleep. Mutterings like the half-words of prayers, or he'd sit up sometimes saying something like the cod-talk of a dream. On the worst nights he'd jump suddenly out of the bed and stand there wondering where he was. He might go outside in his bare feet then and the boy lay awake listening to the retching and heaving as if his stomach was being turned inside-out; seldom enough was there the sound of spew falling on the ground. When he heard the door opening and the cold waddling of feet on the floor he would breathe heavily, pretending to be asleep.

At the beginning of May the doctor's car stopped on the bridge and the horn blew. The boy went over to him when the father told him to. It had rained the night before and puddles of mud had gathered at the bottom of the lane. The doctor stood on the far side of them with his shoes shining and he explained that he couldn't take the car up because the lane was too narrow.

'How is he?' the doctor said.

'Do you not know?' the boy said.

'Yes, but how does he seem to you?'

'He appears to be all stuffed up inside; I'm sure it's sore.'

The doctor held out tablets and the boy walked through the mud to take them.

'He won't go to the hospital for me,' the doctor said. 'Can you do anything to make him?'

'He's a very thick man,' the boy said.

'But he's dying,' the doctor said.

'Yes,' the boy said. 'He told me that.'

When the boy came back the father took the tablets from him and looked at them.

The next day he stayed on in bed for the first time.

He went out to empty the pot himself when the boy was working in the potatoes, moulding them. After a while he asked that the boy's bed be moved into the kitchen or he'd be killed for the want of sleep. With the boy's bed gone he had his own moved over to the window so that he could look out on the land. The smell settled in the room and became heavier with the heat. Flies clustered in, setting up a humming which met the boy when he went in the door. Especially now when they didn't sleep together the boy felt the need to spend the time in the room talking to him. Even when he did go out to work or on the odd time when he went up to the hill he spent the time thinking of things to talk about.

The doctor had to come to the house now and, one day after he left, the father told the boy that the doctor said he shouldn't waste himself talking. 'We'd better not bother any more from now on,' he said. 'It'll let you get time to go up on the hill.' But, now that they weren't talking, now that they were going farther and farther away from each other, the boy needed more to be near him and he hung around outside the window or near the door of the room. Things were growing and noises came in from the outside, but the boy was listening so closely that he could almost hear his father's heart beating.

At the end of May a hole came in the father's back and stuff poured out through it. The doctor showed it to the boy and said that the father should lie on his side from that on and every hour or two the boy should turn him over and empty the stuff into a pot. He was to put him back then lying on the other side. The doctor asked him that day to walk down the lane with him. The lane was dry and he was carrying his galoshes in one hand, his case in the other. Grass was growing in the middle of the lane and hedges were growing across it. The doctor told him he was giving him as much medicine as he could now; any more would kill him, any less wouldn't kill the pain. In a while even what he was giving him wouldn't be enough. He changed the bag and the galoshes to the other hands because the bag was heavier. That time, he said, after the medicines became useless would be the worst. He explained that after a few days of it the nervous system would die of shock and he might sleep till he died. The boy took it all in. He was glad to know what was coming. It was the first time anyone except the father had talked to him like a man.

From that on the days were very silent. The boy didn't work but sat in the kitchen waiting for the hour or two to pass. Then he turned the father over and he leaked slowly into the pot. The hand which he put around the boy's neck was as hard as a rabbit's ribs. One day a piece of paper that the medicine had been wrapped in was lying on the bed. The father lifted it and put it over the pot before the boy took it outside. After that the boy always made sure that he had something to cover it when he was taking it out. When he went back in he might wave a piece of paper at the flies or open the window to let out the smell. He found reasons to stay although the father never talked except when the doctor was there. He just stared out at the land, hardly blinking. On the longest day of the year the boy saw him crying.

'Why don't you say something? A little,' the boy said.

The father didn't let him know that he had heard him.

'I know what it is,' the boy said. 'You want to show that you still have a strong will whatever else fails.'

The father looked at him with a smile which could have been one of fondness or bitterness. The boy didn't know which.

The mowing-machines began. The harvesters were cutting the early hay and silage. The medicines lost their power and soon became no use at all.

Up to this he had borne it or fought it or pretended it wasn't there; now the last while broke

124

him. He couldn't hold the silence and moaned from morning to night, then from night on through till morning. The brain must have been shrinking too the way the rest of him was or he would have been able to stop himself from shouting out the way he did when the boy lifted him to drain him out. At the top of his voice he'd curse or howl. Being moved took so much out of him that he would only be right settled back into a slow moan when the boy had to turn him and start it all over again. He began to look at the boy as if he was causing the pain and when he saw the boy coming towards the bed to lift him he began to whimper and whine. The boy felt it was him he was cursing, that it was against him he was turning his anger. He hated to move him, but the doctor said it'd be worse if he didn't and the boy stayed away from the room, sitting out in the street or in a field, till the time came again and he had to drag himself back, tired from sleepiness and jangling from fear. Neither of them was eating now; the boy's own stomach was turning at the sight of the gold rim on the yolk of an egg, the greasy eyes made by a piece of butter in a teacup. Knocked about by the sleepiness and want of food he thought one night that he heard his father's shouting coming from the top of the hill where the rabbits were and he rushed into the room to be sure he was there. The father was raving. Not out of his sleep; he was awake and shouting. 'Give me them,' he said. 'Turn them. Jesus Christ, they're eating me.' 'They're not,' the boy said, 'you're only dying.' The father seemed to be able to move in the bed as if the strength wasn't coming from himself. He shouted at things to go away and at people to come; he said names of people the boy never knew. Fatty stuff came out of him. And air. And talk as if he was making up for lost time. And still the groans. He kept going crooked in the bed and almost falling out so that the boy had to stay with him all the time, to listen to him. 'Give him tablets to kill him,' the boy said to the doctor; the doctor said it was easily said and went off with his gloves. The nights came down without knowing the time and dawns broke like a punishment to dazzle his eyes. Sitting there in a dawn he could take it no longer. All night the father had kept shouting that they were getting him, that they were killing him and later on in the night, 'Get the gun and be a man, be a man. Give it to them!' The boy wondered if he was asking him to shoot him. He couldn't make sense of it because the father would never have said that and he began to wonder if it could be that the father was really dead and he was listening to his corpse, imagining him to be alive. He had to be away. Away anywhere. Through the blossoming stalks of early potatoes and the thickening corn. Up in the hill with the gun under his arm. Running. Halfway up the hill he shot towards the fort. He scrambled through brush and crawled through tracks under the shadow of blackthorn. He shouted into holes. 'Get away' and emptied cartridge after cartridge into the gaping mouths of the burrows. The sound echoed back out on the mouths of the holes all around. He trampled their mouths with his feet to close them in, his shouting and his stamping and the shots going all around the countryside that was still asleep.

He wakened beside the burrows, not knowing

how long he had slept. The sun was fairly high. His first thought was for his father and he ran down the hill, cartridges thumping against each other in his pockets. The house was quiet when he went in. He still had the gun in his hand when he went into the room. The head was straight on the pillow and the hands were across the chest. There was a look of peace on his face. The boy wondered if he had been right in thinking he was dead all the time. People kneeled, he thought, and he was about to kneel, trying to think of some kind of prayer to say, when the father opened his eyes. The boy stepped back a little; afraid. The father's eyes fixed on him.

'So you made up your mind at last,' the father said.

The boy looked at the gun. Did he mean that ...?

'What?' he said.

'You were up at the fort,' the father said.

'I was. I stayed because the day was getting bright.'

'You had to make up your mind about it,' the father said. 'If you have only ten acres you'll never make out if you're shilly-shallying and...'

He stopped a while. Breathing.

'You'll make out now all right,'' he said.

There was a look of jaded relief on his face. When the boy spoke again he heard his own voice as if it was a man talking.

He said, 'I killed seven. I'm learning to get them two at a time; if they're close together.'

'Where are they?' the father said.

'I left them up there. Nobody buys them. How are you feeling?'

'The pain's gone altogether. It went last night and I feel nothing at all.'

'We'll go to sleep then,' the boy said.

He went towards the door; stopped; feeling he had something else to say. The father was lying back peacefully, sinking into the bed with each breath. He had his eyes closed when he said: 'That girl I saw you looking at; you mightn't be able to get her, but you'll always be able to get one as long as you have a place to bring her to.'

'I'll have that,' the boy said.

He went into the kitchen and lay down on his bed and before he knew he was asleep he wakened and it was evening. Though he wasn't tired at all he lay for a while on the bed looking up at the roof. There was snoring coming from the room and he knew it was all over.

Instead of going into the room he took the gun and went up the hill. This morning and during the past couple of weeks he had been so knocked about that he hadn't noticed that the rabbits had eaten the hay almost to the bottom of the hill. What was left was high and wispy with its seeds falling on the ground. New burrows dotted the hill and the rabbits, almost ignoring him, were scurrying around, their grey patches of tail shaking, their noses shivering. He fired a shot in the air as he went up the hill and he climbed through blooming bluebells into the fort. When the rabbits came out again he fired another shot in the air and watched the bluebells and the grass and the bushes come alive with shivering, frightened tails sinking into the ground. The house, still not whitewashed, looked up from the bottom of the fields. Whether asleep or awake the father would be counting the shots.

Around the countryside there were the last cheers of the evening. Cows were being taken into milking parlours and hot machinery was clattering to a stop, the spikes and thrusting pointed things inside their bellies cracking, cooling, going quiet for the night. The girl got out of the bus at the crossroads and walked down the slope to be hidden by the hill. She had a heavy coat on, though it was the middle of July. Prime weather. With a last shot in the air, he ran back down to the house to see if his father was dead.

The Warmth And The Wine

In Utrecht they talked about war and they seemed to know what it was. They seemed to know about love too, or they said they did. But that was before 1969 when they could remember their parents' memory of 1940.

It was all so new then. There really was a barrel-organ playing tinkling Dutch tunes outside the pancake-house beside the canal and it is true that on the barges which steered between the rising stone walls under the trees there were men who worked in clogs on the fish-scale timber. I noticed the steep Dutch slope of the roofs on old houses and, not so typically Dutch, I saw, one night for the first time in my life, a men-only club, dark-grained with old wood, frosted glass like a hearse in the door. At the time I thought it an anachronism in a progressive society, especially since they didn't actually seem to be doing anything less harmless than sitting around drinking half-pints of beer or long bottles of cheap wine. It was my lack of understanding which prevented me from seeing that it is a logical development in a society which values freedom that men should be free from the company of women if they so desire.

As I imply, I didn't believe that then and when they objected to Nella being with me my behaviour was less well judged than it now would be. Experience, as they say, teaches fools, and my journeyings around the various streets of continental cities in the intervening years would have taught me to treat the rather stout man behind the bar with a little more humour and tolerance.

In fact I think I said something as ridiculous as 'This is bloody ridiculous.'

He treated me with well-worn authority and maturity and waved the back of his hand towards the door. With the palm of his hand outstretched towards Nella he said something in Dutch which I didn't understand.

'He wants us to leave,' she said blushing.

'Tell him I'm a visitor.'

She told him in Dutch and he lifted a glass and cloth as if to indicate that he had work to do.

'*Parlez vous Francais?*' I said to him, becoming, I'm sure, angry. He didn't, obviously, because he said something to Nella. She answered him with her voice shaking but he ignored her and, instead of answering, indicated to one of the men at the tables that he had heard his request for another drink.

'He wants you to leave even though you're a tourist' Nella said. 'I think we should.'

She was, in many ways, a shy and reticent girl, Nella, and I thought at the time that he was taking advantage of this weakness in her. I made my views clear to him, though we did have difficulty in communicating, but he was quite adamant about his principles and I did end up in the street without having had anything to drink.

Perhaps it was the quite violent nature of my ejection which led us to talk about war in the pan-cake-house. My anger had subsided and Nella was laughing at how serious I still was about it all; the wine was good enough (better quality wines since then have not tasted quite so new) and the cosiness of the architecture and the atmos-phere in the pillared cellar with its tiled tables helped to soothe away the harrowing nature of my experience. When we talked about the war then, it was about something outside us; something forgotten or half-remembered.

'Here,' she said, 'we live in danger.'

'Well, not now,' I said.

'It's always there. We live with it. We learn to live with it not hurting us.'

This was typical of what I found to be the state of mind of young Hollanders at the time; they all seemed curiously obsessed with their non-existent vulnerability. In discussions over tea or beer during the seminar — it was a seminar of young scientists on whether science should adopt some thought disciplines from the humanities (I deal in rocks myself) — this became abundantly clear to me. A few Dutch colleagues felt it was due to their historical consciousness of being surrounded by powers greater than themselves. None of them, however, for all their learning, phrased it quite so quaintly as Nella: 'We're like this,' she said. She prodded with her knife the pancake she was eating. It was one of those large pancakes (which haven't reached Ireland yet) which are doubled over to enclose cooked apples or some such steamy

132

thing. 'Germany, France, England: if they disagree again, we're the apples. It only takes a new idea or a retreat to an old idea. It's always ideas which start wars, and the ideas which end them take too long to think out.'

'But surely,' I said, 'you can't exclude knowledge.'

'What knowledge?'

'Quest. Ideas involve risk and the pursuit of ideas is the pursuit of knowledge.'

'Both my parents were killed by the Nazis; is that the sort of knowledge we should all have?'

'I'm sorry,' I said to her when I saw how angry she was.

'What the hell,' she said, with her unfamiliar mastery of English slang, 'it's life. We're not an island people.'

I think I felt guilty and a little envious.

'Why should we talk about war,' she said. 'I'm warm and happy and you buy me wine and a meal.'

'I'm sure that if I didn't somebody else would.'

'Would what?' she said, laughing, and I remember the whiteness of her teeth on the lip of the glass. I must admit that I found her company fresh, mainly because she often surprised me with some toss of the head or a loose turn of her body which betrayed an openness I was not then accustomed to.

'Someone else would buy you a meal if I didn't. Penury is easily recognisable.'

'What's penury?'

It took me a deal of time to explain that it wasn't difficult to know a student on sight and that there were many men who, when alone, would buy one of them a meal in return for their company.

133

'But they're not Irish,' she said.

'Does it make a difference?'

'Big,' she said, and she put her hands on her very blonde hair and pushed her elbows backwards so that she bulged in front.

'Why?' I think I was flattered.

'Because I love the Irish. In some ways you're all so innocent.' Her laugh was high-pitched with delight and, I think it's true to say, affection.

'Innocent?' I said. 'Whatever we are we're not innocent.'

'Show me the Belgian, the Frenchman, the German who would have done what you did at the club tonight. And show me the Czech or the whatever among those big wigs' — she said it as two words — 'at that seminar of yours who is so curious and obsessed by war as you are.'

It was totally untrue and she knew it but, because I had grown relatively fond of her, I didn't mind her teasing me about it. The fact that she couldn't find a real fault with which to satirise me confirmed in my mind that I was an attractive person to her and the 'war-joke', as we came to call it, provided a useful centre-point to which we could return when other avenues of communication had been closed or when the effects of the wine and the warmth dulled our desire to pursue more intelligent subjects. It was an extremely pleasant evening and the air in the cellar was clean.

I can't remember why we began to talk about my hotel but it was probably in response to some query of hers. I didn't mind, of course, telling her that I wouldn't have stayed in it had I been bearing the expense myself, and it was probably due to the novelty of it that I felt it necessary to tell her about it and particularly about the proliferation of towels in the bathroom — five in all.

'Whatever for?' she said, her voice high with hardly concealed mirth.

'I can't think,' I said. 'If I were of a different biological structure it might be explained by having one for each orifice.'

I remember distinctly that she counted on her fingers before bursting into laughter. Or maybe it wasn't on her fingers but I am certain she counted.

We talked about Ireland and its legends and I related our history in a ridiculously romantic style which bore little resemblance to the reality of it. The night wore on and the crowds thinned in the cellar and our conversation became sporadic, yet imbued with a quality of stillness and calm. In one of those pauses when she seemed physically to soak up ease, she put her hands up to the ropes which webbed the walls and ceiling and it seemed as if the whole interior quivered from her touch. Maybe it was because I had drunk too much but I remember thinking what a marvellous physical specimen she was — big and buxom with a body so fluid that even those feelings and thoughts which should be concealed seemed to find expression in the smallest movement of a shoulder or in the manner in which she fingered the ropes over her head. It was as if the wine had washed away all her reticence and what was left was the true Nella emotionally naked in front of me.

I said something about beauty in the abstract sense and, misinterpreting my meaning, she said 'Do you think I'm beautiful?' We discussed beauty and the different forms it took and I told her that, yes, given my predeliction for the seemingly contradictory elements of strength and vulnerability, I would say she was a beautiful woman. She was so pleased that she nestled into herself with a sigh of happiness and her hand came up to caress the glass.

'Many people tell me that, but I find it hard to believe. People tell lies sometimes.'

She thought for a minute after she said that and, for the first time, her face seemed to cloud over with sadness. She was turning the wine with her wrist, observing the changes in its sparkle. She took a deep breath and lifted the glass to her eye. A button opened on her blouse. She closed one eye and looked at me through the wine.

'Where do you go from here?' she said.

I was beginning to tell her of my plans for my career when she said: 'I meant tonight.'

I explained that I was to have a drink with some of my colleagues in one of their rooms and, out of courtesy, I asked her what she intended to do for the remainder of the evening.

'Who cares?' she said. 'It's just an evening. These colleagues, as you call them, will only men colleagues be there?'

'No.'

'And the men colleagues' wives?'

'I suppose so.'

'Then nobody would notice me and I'd like to go with you. The evening's been such fun and I'd like to see how big intelligent wigs live.'

I pointed out at that stage that I was married and that my wife hadn't come with me to Holland.

'Okay,' she said.

'I wanted to tell you,' I said.

'You're so honest,' she said. 'That's what I love about you Irish.'

I told her I wanted her to know that, lest we misunderstand each other; in retrospect it was a clumsy thing to say, but she didn't appear to mind. Made easy by our new understanding we dallied by the table and the urgency of my previous appointment became less sharp.

I have never since visited that pancake-house, nor, for that matter, have I ever gone back to that part of Utrecht. It may be the wine beside me as I write which makes me somewhat maudlin about it, but its leatherette seats, its tiled table, the wooden condiment containers and its square brick pillars will always be clear in my mind. The steps up to the street were of rough stone and as we neared the top, the notes from the barrel-organ came down to meet us.

'He's still playing,' I said.

'He has to earn his living.'

'He keeps the street alive.'

'This street would be alive without him,' Nella said. 'All night there's the water of the canal and the chains jingle if the wind blows.'

'And barges, I suppose, all night.'

'You don't need barges to have life. There are trees and bridges and sky.'

There was rain on the cobbled footpaths — the first I had seen there. I was without a jacket and she opened her umbrella over me. Even the rain seemed new; it dripped from the trees and livened the water of the canal; across the canal the organ-grinder had pulled out a striped cover over where he stood. Gradually the notes began to fade and she linked my arm as we passed a break in the

137

chain, explaining with a laugh that she was afraid
we might lurch into the canal. For a long time
we said nothing. There came singing from a church
covered with ivy which the lights from inside
shone through. It was one of the most beautiful
things I have ever seen but I felt that any comment
would break the simple rhythm of our walking and
the quietness inside me which I now know can be
attributed to the wine. I took off my tie sometime then and rolled it before putting it in my
pocket because, though rain was pouring down, it
was warm. Occasionally a cyclist passed, bent
against the weather; a few cars splashed along the
cobbles.

'Are you long married?' she asked me after a
while. 'Do you like it?'

'Five or six years, I suppose.'

'You must have married young; have you any
children?'

'A boy.'

'Are Irishmen like Dutchmen. Do they like
boys?'

'Yes. Well, not all, I'm sure.'

'Your tie's going to fall out.'

'How careless of me.'

We broke from the canal; passed a café where
they sold ornaments and, strangely, a pet-shop
which was open even at that hour. There was an
old black man inside feeding a macaw and I stopped
to look at him. She walked slowly on as if she
hadn't noticed I had stopped and I had to run to
catch the shelter of her umbrella. When I reached
her she raised the umbrella to my height and
slipped her arm around me without saying a
word. She stopped at the railings around a statue

to the war dead.

'I'm not religious,' she said, 'but I know that here I meet my father.'

'Terrible time,' I said rather stupidly.

We sat on the railings in the rain. We were in the middle of a kind of square which contained an indescribable maze of pedestrian crossings, cycle paths and road-junctions. The old was beside the new; brightly-lit boutiques with leaning models in the windows contrasted with the vegetable shops and private houses, brown and dark and old.

'This place is so . . .'

'How high is your room?' she said.

'Where?'

'In the hotel.'

'High enough to see Utrecht. It's so integrated; old Dutch buildings and in the distance high office-blocks that mingle with the houses.'

'They *are* houses, or what people call houses. We don't remember Holland.'

'Cosmopolitan.'

'Like what I said about war. You're lucky to live in Ireland. We're a hotch-potch; that's what you get for questing ideas.'

She put all of her umbrella over me and held her face up to the rain. I don't know why I didn't insist that she'd catch a cold; maybe I knew, even then, that she wasn't the kind to take good advice from anyone. The rain dribbled from her hair and gathered in the folds of her creased eyes. When she turned to me again her face was dewed and her short hair was streaked where the light shone on it. I add nothing to the conversation which then took place as I add nothing to any of the incidents which happened. They are as I remember them and I remember them accurately. What now appears fanciful did, in my inebriated state at the time, appear to me quite normal.

'I'm a water-nymph,' she said.

'Good for you.'

'I'm serious I sometimes do this even in winter. In summer I am a gypsy and I go places and live in a tent.'

'A novel idea.'

'No, no, no. Novel ideas are making office-houses. Old ideas are living in tents, putting your face to the rain.'

I'm afraid I succumbed to the temptation to remind her that she'd catch a cold.

'Cold,' she said, speading her arms to the rain. 'Cold. The Irishman is drunk and he's afraid of the cold. Do you know why I put my face to the rain? To keep me from crying. Yes. To keep me from crying. I let nature make my tears and you will think that they're not mine. This is my Inter-continental with the same picture on the same wall in every room, three beds for one person and five towels in the bathroom.'

'I don't know what you mean.'

'Of course you don't; you're Irish; that's why I love you.'

I thought from the way she looked at me that she meant a personal love.

'We're all descended from The Celts, I suppose,' I said inaccurately.

She laughed and hugged me tightly to herself and I felt her dampness through my shirt.

'Maybe I should leave you at your flat,' I said. 'It's getting late.'

'No, I have to see the big intelligent wigs; my father might have been a wig but I was reared on a farm.'

'You won't misbehave if I bring you?'

She threw her arms to the sky and danced around me, her feet splashing water on to my clothes. 'No,' she said, 'I promise.' She hugged me again and took the umbrella and as she calmed down she laid her face against my chest. After a while she lifted her head; the raindrops were still on her cheeks.

'Not this summer,' she said. 'I'm not a gypsy now. I stay in my room and I have a job — well you know that, because that's where you met me. I don't mind as long as I don't spend summer on the farm. Farms are for boys.'

She went out from under the umbrella again and stepped across the low railing. She sat on it and took off her shoes and walked in her bare feet up the steps leading to the statue. It was the usual type of statue with a fellow in heroic posture carrying a gun and looking into the distance as if into the mystical future. The water came around her feet; she was in no hurry, her head bowed with the kind of reverence which the normal reserve for a sacrament. When she came to the level of the statue she put the soles of her shoes together in front of her face as if making an offering of them. Then she slowly extended her arms with a shoe in each hand and she moved, as if in a ceremony, towards the statue. When she was against it she folded her arms around it and stayed there, I don't know how long, oblivious of the rain. In time she began to hum a Dutch tune which I had heard on numerous occasions from the barrel-organ. It was a low humming like the rising sound of a boat in the distance and it seemed to come from her without any effort on her part. She stopped and put her head to the statue and she lay against it as if she was unable to support her own weight. After a while she moved backwards, her head still bowed, and put on her shoes again. Nothing she had done had been impulsive or wild in the ordinary meaning of those words. She turned and looked down at me.

'You're puzzled,' she said. 'It's my religion. Like my religion?'

'But religion's about God,' I said, 'not statues.'

'How do you know? Religion's about people — about easing the troubles of this life.'

Somewhat irrelevantly I said, 'He's looking into the future.'

'He's looking at the possible.'

I don't know what way I looked at her; I must have been staring because she began to laugh. She came running down the watery steps, jumped across the railing and threw her arms around me.

'Don't worry,' she said, 'it means nothing. It's just that here, more than anywhere else, I can be myself. Come on. We have wigs to see.'

The most amazing aspect of the entire incident, looking back on it, is that at no time, as far as I can remember, was I aware of anyone looking at us. I know there were people on the street at the time but I cannot say whether they stopped; maybe they even gathered into a crowd. Cars, I'm sure, passed, but I don't know if their occupants even noticed the strangeness of our behaviour. Drunks are no more common in Holland than they are in Ireland and yet, if a couple behaved as we did in the vicinity of a statue in Dublin, I'm certain they would attract no mean attention. It is a measure of our inebriation that I didn't even consider what people might think.

In any case, we went across the traffic-lanes to the street which led to my hotel. She was against me and she soaked into me through my shirt. We didn't talk but occasionally she began to hum to herself the same Dutch tune — a kind of tripping tune, in no way mournful. We came near the canal again and there was a smell, uncommonly like silage, from a passing barge and we walked through a long pedestrian tunnel with dull cobbles which hadn't been shined by the rain. Sometimes, going through it, we stopped like partners in a dance and leaned against its wall; then, without any signal whatsoever, we moved off again. She began to hum the tune again.

'What's that tune?'

'It's Dutch. We sing it at celebrations; we put on false noses and faces and we are clowns, yes? Then we dance and we touch our noses and faces and we sing it.'

'How charming and quaint.'

'Like your Guy Fawkes, yes?'

'Guy Fawkes is England.'

'I'm sorry.'

When we came out of the tunnel again the rain was lightening. She gave me the umbrella and shook out her wet hair with her hands. I can honestly say that I looked on her then with pure affection unaccompanied by desire. At least I would like to think that it was so. The town was changing; we were coming out of the old town and the buildings were becoming higher; the sound of the incessant night-traffic of the new town was in the distance. We talked in spurts like slow heartbeats; sometimes just footsteps and her breathing or the little humming which she kept repeating. Like our Guy Fawkes, she had said. Footfalls — an extra one if we met someone — and then more talk. Thought — like now; it was a time for thought and even then I was a thinking man. My mood then is my mood now; my study is quiet like the street and the wine is helping me to be quiet. I could go outside now and walk down the avenue of trees to the bright lights on the road and I could truly believe to myself that I was walking through the tunnel and out of the old town and into the brightness of the city's busy traffic. I can still believe that I am the younger man and that he is me. My footsteps would be the same, Nella's beside me. Probably now Nella is asleep. We could walk on — walked on.

When we reached the traffic she became gay and light again. The rectangular windows of the Intercontinental were over the roofs of the houses; the street was full of Citroens and Dafs and boxey cars from all over Europe. She ran on to the pedestrian crossing opposite the hotel and put up both her hands to stop the oncoming traffic. She ran towards the hotel and I walked after her. When I came to its forecourt she was running over the rubber rectangles which activated the glass doors, opening each one as she passed, chuckling and exclaiming and singing to herself, spanging from door to door, water jetting from under her feet into the foyer.

'Come on,' she shouted excitedly, 'and help me.'

Naturally I declined and she followed me into the foyer and into the lift.

She stood in the corner of the lift leaning her still wet hair against the shiny metal. She was laughing happily and she began to sing the words of the tune she had been humming.

Mein where is my face face?
Mein where is my nose?'

It frightened me momentarily when she plummeted down along the corner and came to rest on the floor. I thought she had fainted but she sighed and said: 'I'm so happy — so happy.

Mein where is my face face?
Mein where is my nose?'

We went towards the room where my colleagues and I had planned to have the drink together. The door was closed and we listened for the sound of conversation. It would be false of me to attempt to describe how we discovered that my colleagues had long since broken up and gone to bed; the fact is that I don't remember; were I a writer I might be able to re-create the incident in a fictional way but I have no such skill and the only memory I have from that point in time is of my anxiety— and this may sound terrible, but it's true — that I might have to leave her back across the city to wherever she had her room. The rain had become heavy again on the window at the far end of the corridor.

The remainder of the story is rather embarrassing for me to relate but I feel that it is necessary that I should, if I am to know why I sit here in the middle of a hot summer night writing because I want to think and thinking because I cannot sleep. Why, after so many years, should I again and again think about Nella? If I could blame myself for it there might be some sort of expiation in it, but the fact was that I met her by pure chance, that my intention was never other than cordial companionship and that she did come to my hotel completely unasked. Even if I had asked her to come to my room I might have cause for guilt, but, instead, I signalled to her to sit on the floor against the door of my colleague's room.

I sat against the opposite wall of the corridor and put on my tie again.

'It must be over,' I said.

'No big wigs; all wigs asleep.'

'We may as well sit here till the rain eases before you go,' I said.

'Thank you for fighting for me.'

'Fighting?'

'In the men's club.'

'Oh.'

We sat for a while, both of us thinking. Eventually she lay down on the carpeted floor of the corridor.

'The rain won't ease,' she said.

'We'll wait and see.'

'On nights like this in the war,' she said 'soldiers felt safer. Those were the nights when they raped women or made love as the case may be.'

I don't remember whether or not I answered her. She began to hum to herself again, thoughtfully, stopping now and again, looking at me and starting again. I think I tried to look as determined and as severe as possible and I remained sitting where I was while she went down to the end of the long corridor and followed the raindrops with her fingers on the glass. I was looking at her when she turned around and said: 'I want to sleep with you.'

I didn't answer because one doesn't conduct such conversations along a large corridor of occupied rooms. She came back to me.

'Did you hear me?' she said. 'I really meant it.'

'But I told you I was married.'

'I said that was okay.'

'One doesn't do such things. Not in civilised countries.'

'But it's still raining,' she said, 'and it's a long way back to my room. One doesn't, as you say, put people out in rain in civilised countries.'

She walked up and down angrily, talking to herself, sitting on the floor and pouting. I told her she was already wet and that, in any case, she had her umbrella. She lay down on the floor and began to cry and, though I knew that I was being quite callous to her, I resolved to be unrelenting. I cannot explain why I didn't leave her there and go to my room; maybe I was afraid she might cry aloud and draw the attention of the entire hotel, maybe it was kindness on my part, or maybe it was simply because I didn't think of such a course.

'I'm soaking,' she said, looking down at herself, 'and I only want a place to sleep.'

She took off her jacket and left it beside her and she loosened the top of her skirt. Her hands moved quickly to the buttons of her blouse and I relented, fearing what might happen if someone were to come out of the lift suddenly and discover me in the corridor with a half-clad young girl. My acute feeling of discomfort as we walked along to my room can be imagined; it was a feeling never since equalled in any similar situation and it causes me some pain, even now, to remember it.

It is difficult for me too, because it must appear comic and undignified, to confess that I undressed in the bathroom with all the crockery and five towels. I would like to relate that I took her and made love to her in the light of the window but I was so inexperienced then that I actually shouted from the bathroom, when I had donned my pyjamas, to ask if it was all right if I should come in. She said it was and when I went in she was leaning back in the armchair, apparently comfortable in her sopping clothes, her outstretched feet on top of her jacket on the radiator. I asked her if she was all right and she said she was fine and I indicated that she could sleep in whichever of the other two beds she wished. Before I got into bed I turned out the light. Her hair was shining in the light of the window and the highlight on her nose and forehead made dark hollows of her eyes. Unsure of whether she wished to undress or not, I turned towards the wall when I got into bed.

She sat there for a long time before she got up, turned on the light again and went back towards the window.

'Do you have to go to work in the morning?' I said.

'Yes, I have to be up early.'

'Well, lest I sleep, make the bed before you leave.'

'Why make beds?'

'Because the hotel charges for the number of beds occupied.'

'Then why do they have three beds? It's stupid having three beds. One person can't sleep in three

148

beds.'

'Sometimes families might require such accommodation.'

'Families! Families!'

It was in frustration that I turned towards her and, quite by chance, I assure you — because I had not heard any movement from her — I saw her standing utterly naked on the floor. Her body glistened from where the rain had soaked through her clothes and she had her arms behind her head as she had had them in the pancake-house. She resembled the type of statue I have often since seen in Rome or Athens or in the parks in Stockholm. She was a thing of rare beauty; a water nymph, as she had called herself. I couldn't turn away and it would have been ridiculous to close my eyes. The fact that she was so unselfconscious seemed to me then to be something very rare. She came walking towards me with her arms outstretched as she had approached the statue.

'If I sleep in another bed,' she said, 'and make it in the morning then, when you leave, okay, someone will have to sleep in it without the sheets being laundered. It doesn't seem an unselfish thing to do. It's not responsible and social.'

She bent close to me where I lay.

'Your wife will never know,' she said. She took my head in her hands and directed my face towards her. I believe I actually began to cry.

'I don't know who your wife is,' she said, 'and there must be millions and millions of people in Ireland and even if I visited Ireland sometime I would never tell anyone. As you say, I assure you.'

Her frame blurred in the tears in my eyes.

'Millions,' I said, illogically. I moved my head to wipe my eye on her thumb.

'Even to nobody in Holland I would tell,' she said. She lifted my head and pressed it tightly against her breast and I closed my eyes so that I couldn't see the hair between her legs.

'I love you, Nella,' I said. 'Please go away.'

It was her turn to cry; she sank onto my face on the pillow and gradually slid to the floor. Her head still rested on my pillow and I put my hand on the back of her neck to prevent her head from falling to the floor. Her hair was drying but when I put my hand around to touch her face her eyes dampened the palm of my hand. For me there was no longer anything to cry about and I found the strength to console her and finger her face. Had I taken her in my arms then and made love to her with every fibre of my being it would have changed nothing because I was already changed. That, I think, is the understanding which comes to me tonight for the first time; the action itself was unimportant because, even before I had entered my room, she, like the statue, had shown me the possible — that it is possible to be tolerant to things you disagree with — and the man I am now was born an hour after midnight on a wet street in the old town of Utrecht.

For her the change was probably less severe because she didn't have beliefs which could be altered by it. It probably went no farther than the deep sense of humiliation with which her crying reproached me.

'It's time we went to sleep,' I said.

Her head slid from the pillow onto my sheet.

'You must be a Catholic,' she said. 'That's why

you're not religious; you have a closed mind.'

'I'm married. Being Catholic has nothing to do with it.'

'That's why you're so unkind.'

She must have sat there crying for nearly an hour. Her body dried and she raised herself a little so that her elbows were resting on my bed. I rubbed her back without the merest feeling of desire and thought left my mind; I became conscious of the traffic in the night-city and my mind wandered over the city outside the window with its box-houses and box-cars making mockery of the black man with the macaw and the clogged men on the barges of the canal, making a mockery even of the monument in the rain. Although I say that those were my conscious thoughts then, it is probably truer to say that it is my present view of what my thoughts might have been; maybe it is more honest to say that the uppermost thought in my mind then was that the ordeal was over and that, in my own view, I had triumphed over adversity. Or maybe they were just about Nella because I cannot recall that I had any other feeling than one of at least relative peace.

Her sobbing subsided and she got to her feet. Now I could look at her without embarrassment.

'I'm sorry,' she said, 'you're not unkind.'

'Turn off the light,' I said.

When she turned it off she dallied by the switch. The light from the window gave her face a strangely comic look.

'You must love your wife terribly,' she said.

'Of course I do.'

She got into the bed nearest to me and she rustled and tugged at the clothes before finally settling into position.

'What age is the kid?' she said.

'He's two. My wife worked for a few years after we were married: it wasn't for the money or anything; she didn't want to be tied — that's all.'

'Nice age,' she said. 'My brother was a kid that age when I was born. Dutchmen are like Irishmen. They like boys. Especially foster-parents like boys.'

I don't think I answered her, and, though I've gone over our conversations many times, I can't think of anything I might have said.

'My brother's big now.' She laughed at that. 'Of course that's how it should be when I'm this age. He works the farm at home but they sent me to be a student to try and make something out of me and in summer . . . It's biology I'm studying. I don't know anything about rocks. Rocks must be interesting.'

I didn't answer her then because I was going over the evening.

'That's why they give me the job in the kitchen in summer at the Academy because I study biology. Why did you talk to me?'

'Where?'

'At the table.'

'I don't know. I'm still a little drunk so I can't think; I suppose it was because I liked you.'

'That's nice.'

From the inward sound of her voice I knew that she was happy. She began to make popping sounds with her mouth and tap herself with her fingers under the bedclothes. I tried to sleep and, momentarily, I did imagine myself somewhere above the Irish Sea in the clouds; there was no hum of engines and I seemed to be outside of myself, watching myself impassively. At that moment when total ease might have taken me, the rain beat heavily on the window-pane and she sat up in bed to look at it whispering down the glass. She was making happy clucking noises as if conversing with the raindrops.

'The rain's all around us,' she said. 'It's much of a pity we're not out there.'

Go to sleep. We have to get up in the morning.'

'Goodnight,' she said, lying back. 'Thank you for the night.'

'Goodnight.'

There was only her breathing as if her body was no longer in the room. It became so deep and heavy that I thought she had gone to sleep. It jolted me, therefore, when she laughed quietly to herself and, in a deep-down chuckling voice, began to sing:

> 'Mein where is my face face?
> Mein where is my nose?'

She stopped, seeming to lapse into thought, sighed, and said, "Wouldn't everything be beautiful if only half of the men in the world could love.'

It was the last thing she said before she went to sleep.

Sleep didn't come to me. My head was reeling from the effects of the wine. The room was warm with a permanent smell of perfume. Everything seemed to be whispering: her breathing; the susurration of rain on the window; the faint squeak of wheels somewhere in the hotel; the low hum-tone of the traffic; the weak breath of the cistern in the bathroom with the five towels. A stealthy bubble whistled in the radiator where her jacket hung drying. But the loudest whispering came from myself: not a prayer or any kind of dialogue with the God who forgives and soothes — no whisper of thanks for His graces. If it was God who was whispering to me He was whispering through the mouth of the statue in the rain — the statue with the fixed stare, looking for life which, when seen, would be ended. Her shoes were on his shoulders, on her God's shoulders, and the voice of her God whispered to me that there was a life outside life as I knew it and that I should grasp it while it was still there. Such was the effect of the night that I imagined that there was even a kind of life in this room with its coloured print and its three beds and a naked woman oblivious of the world. Not an unpeaceful life and not one which could be located anywhere, but a kind of presence in the perfumed room which hung like a layer somewhere over my eyes. Those are my sensibilities as they were then and I have tried not to impose my present views upon them. Hallucinatory experience can very easily be recalled with gross exaggeration and I am prepared to allow for this, but I am certain that I was glad when I felt myself beginning to succumb to the more tranquil effects of the wine because I knew that, whatever the morning would bring, it would be at least partly related to reality and normality. When eventually I fell asleep I slept soundly. It must surely be present circumstances which make me imagine that I dreamt I was at home and that there were soldiers at the bottom of my drive. One of them came over to me with a smile and kissed me and I opened my eyes and she was standing there in the room. Morning was coming. She bent and kissed me again and I'm certain she said 'I'll see you.' In my half-sleeping state I may have put out my hand to touch her hair or something like that — some indefinite little gesture of half-approbation. There was the sound of soft feet on the carpet and the closing of a door before I went back to sleep.

When I wakened I had a headache. The rain had stopped. I was sweating because the radiator hadn't been turned off and the hot Dutch sun was shining in the window. During that day and on other days of that week I imagined myself not as impressive in my speeches as I would like to have been and, in consequence, found the remainder of the seminar somewhat disturbing. On these days Nella never came from the kitchen to wait on the tables and all I saw of her was a single fleeting glimpse when a door was opened. She had her back to me and she was mixing something. The door swung closed and she never knew that I saw her again. It didn't rain any more that week and on the journey to Amsterdam I found the coarse rear of Dutch farmhouses not at all offensive nor the regularity of their rectangular grass-paddocks at all disquieting. I need not describe my first flight out of Holland except to say it was an excellent flight totally uninfluenced by any atmospheric disturbance.

I have often thought since then that had our final parting been true exactly to the relationship we had she might not have haunted me so; so many things remind me of her. Rarely, for example, do I fly over the irregular townscape of Dublin without thinking of her; or new things: yes, new things somehow recall her to me — like the new sweater the kid bought yesterday with 'University of Illinois' emblazoned on it even though he has never been outside Ireland. Or sometimes, like tonight, it's the warmth and the wine; it is unusually hot for Ireland and I sat on in this quiet study waiting for the kid to come in. By the time he came I had drunk some; the wife was in bed and I intended to talk to him — just chat. He mentioned the heat of the night and blamed it for his tiredness. True, even now in the dark hours, I can almost feel the heat of yesterday's sun rising from the ground. The air is the air of that room and down at the lights of the road there is a flesh-statue of a soldier, furtive under a tree. If a car comes he will move out like a robot, wait till a garda checks the car for bombs and move in again. It causes me some amusement that the possible physical manifestation of the soldier who kissed me should turn out to be like a figure from an old-fashioned weather-guide with a man and a woman at the door. In saying this I do not want to be facetious about our soldiery; they are necessary if we are to keep this wretched business from the North from spilling into the Republic and if I am not to be worried about my wife's or my kid's safety when their household or scholastic duties take them into the centre of the town (a bomb exploded there some time ago, killing some number of poor fellows from the country). What I am saying is that their frequent presence there (a bothersome presence when one has to join a queue of cars at the bottom of one's own driveway even if one is going on the shortest of journeys) may have combined with the other elements I have mentioned to produce in me the unprecedented urge to reach out to Nella, to capture her spirit as a grey old priest might do and put it in a bottle where it could disturb only if allowed to.

Because I must admit that she does disturb me. Otherwise why should I have spent the early night walking from room to room and why should I be here in this silent house with a glass of claret in a hot dawn? And there is a dawn rich as the claret. The rain has stopped dripping from the trees that arch over the drive and the birds are getting up to sing. Over the town the sky is brightening and the mist is making islands of the hills. In an hour the sun will scatter the mist and the night-neon-signs of the town and then the huddles of dark brown houses will become visible. Before this happens I hope to be in bed and I hope that, as I go to sleep, I will be happy that in writing this story I have done something to make amends for the way I treated her — that I have performed my expiation. Even if she never reads this I will have done my part in letting her know that I still remember her and that I have often repeated to myself every word, every gesture, every incident which took place on our journey out of the old town of Utrecht and into the bright lights of the new city; that twice in London and once in Hamburg when I should have had more to think about in night-city hotel rooms I saw her face again as clearly as I had seen it that night and I thought, with some little regret, on the hurt that was in it. Perhaps it is to ease the hurt that I want the world to know that she did touch me; that I was touched by her. Because she helped me achieve maturity and fullness of personality; to free the patterns of my thoughts. I would never now, for example, become embroiled in an incident like that which happened in the men-only clubs; neither would I ever again handle with such indelicacy an incident

157

such as that which occurred between us. So that
even if she is now married I want it to be known,
I want her to know, that I owe her something; that
I want to make amends. I hold my present moral
views with the same conviction as I did then and if,
sometimes on my lecture-tours of the Continent,
I have strayed from the path of these convictions,
I have sought and obtained spiritual pardon as
soon as possible after my return; and I want her
to know that I now think that, had I acted in this
way in her case, it might, in the end, have been a
more humane thing to do.